"PLOTTING SOMETHING?" DEVLIN ASKED HER.

Gabrielle gave him a mischievous look. "Do I look like I'm plotting something?"

He turned her to face him, holding her arms lightly. "You look—he traced two fingers over her mouth—"tempting as hell." His eyes had darkened. He gazed at her but made no move to kiss her. Yet.

Devlin knew exactly what he did to women. No man who looked like he did could be unaware of his power. He was a master of the game, a maestro of smooth moves. Had he ever let a woman get to him? Gabrielle seriously doubted it. She ardently wanted to give him back some of what he dished out.

Could she? What if the seducer became the seduced? If she could cloud his thinking, then she'd have the upper hand. The challenge was irresistible. "You know what Oscar Wilde said," she murmured, deliberately reaching for a husky whisper.

Devlin drew her closer. Despite her best efforts, her heartbeat sped up. A sizzle of tension stretched its sultry tentacles between them.

"No, what did he say?" he asked, his voice as husky as hers.

She lifted her chin and met his gaze with a smoky challenge in her own. "The only way to get rid of a temptation is to yield to it."

He smiled, the smooth, sexy smile she knew made women want to rip off their clothes for him. And dammit, it had the same effect on her. . . .

WHAT ARE *LOVESWEPT* ROMANCES?

They are stories of true romance and touching emotion. We believe those two very important ingredients are constants in our highly sensual and very believable stories in the LOVE-SWEPT line. Our goal is to give you, the reader, stories of consistently high quality that may sometimes make you laugh, sometimes make you cry, but are always fresh and creative and contain many delightful surprises within their pages.

Most romance fans read an enormous number of books. Those they truly love, they keep. Others may be traded with friends and soon forgotten. We hope that each LOVESWEPT romance will be a treasure—a "keeper." We will always try to publish

LOVE STORIES YOU'LL NEVER FORGET
BY AUTHORS YOU'LL ALWAYS REMEMBER

The Editors

ON THIN ICE

EVE GADDY

BANTAM BOOKS

NEW YORK · TORONTO · LONDON · SYDNEY · AUCKLAND

ON THIN ICE

A Bantam Book / September 1997

ISBN 0-553-44579-0

Published simultaneously in the United States and Canada

Bantam Books are published by Bantam Books, a division of Bantam Dou-
bleday Dell Publishing Group, Inc. Its trademark, consisting of the words
"Bantam Books" and the portrayal of a rooster, is Registered in U.S.
Patent and Trademark Office and in other countries. Marca Registrada.
Bantam Books, 1540 Broadway, New York, New York 10036.

PRINTED IN THE UNITED STATES OF AMERICA

OPM   10 9 8 7 6 5 4 3 2 1

For Sheli, Roz, and Trana,
the best critique partners in the world.
And for Elizabeth Barrett,
the best editor.

ONE

It was obscenely expensive, totally impractical, and the most gorgeous thing Gabrielle Rousseau had ever seen. Soft and silky, it flowed over her skin like a caress, whispering, "You know you want me."

With a wicked smile Gabrielle slipped out of the emerald-green nightgown and redressed, layering her sensible tan suit over her frivolous lace bra and panties. Placing the pièce de résistance on top of the rainbow offering of underthings, she abandoned the dressing room before practicality set in.

She was worth it, Gabrielle reminded herself. After the fight she'd been through, she deserved a perk. Winning a case was an incredible, though fleeting, high. Lingerie lasted longer.

Partner. She tossed her head up, seeing the title in her mind's eye. Each victory brought her dream closer. And this particular triumph, the seemingly

impossible task of proving Mike McDermott innocent of murder, had given her an adrenaline rush
that could only be compared to—So far, she hadn't
found anything to compare it to. *Fast track, choke on
my dust*, she thought. She was on the warp-speed
track now, phasers on stun—

The emerald nightgown slid from the top of
the heap of clothing in her arms. Gabrielle grabbed
for it, missed, and tripped over a display, landing
amongst the kaleidoscope of lingerie that pooled at
a man's feet.

Cursing her clumsiness under her breath, she
didn't look up but scrambled to retrieve her haul.
Hopefully he'd go away and leave her alone, not
try to help and make her feel like even more of a
klutz. No such luck. He dropped down beside her,
and she found herself gazing at richly black kid
leather Italian loafers. Exactly the type of shoes a
prosperous businessman would wear.

Or a successful attorney.

Lord, please don't let it be anyone I know, she
prayed. Not that there was anything wrong with
going to a lingerie shop on her lunch hour. But as
one of Christian, Gilmer & Simmons's hottest and,
she hoped, fastest rising trial lawyers, she took
pains to present an entirely professional image. A
weakness for fancy lingerie wasn't something she
wanted printed on her resume.

Gabrielle raised her head and stared into gray
eyes fringed with thick brown lashes. Straight
gold-blond hair fell to the collar of his navy pin-

striped suit. A patented knock-your-socks-off smile kicked up at one corner of his mouth and a skimpy black lace bra dangled from his long, graceful fingers.

"Excuse me. I believe this is yours." His deep voice held laughter in check, though amusement glimmered in his eyes.

Warmth flooded her face, spreading over her neck and chest. Paralyzed, she stared at the blond god in front of her and wanted to sink into the floor. "No, I—you—Oh, never mind."

So much for her famed ability to think on her feet. She snatched at the bra, catching the lace on the clasp of his watchband. Yanking on the elastic strap, she tried to untangle them but only managed to create a snarl, much like the effect she had on a fishing line whenever she touched one.

"It won't—I can't—" Increasingly frustrated, she fought with the bra, which by now had taken on a life of its own and wrapped itself around his arm like an amorous python. "Oh, damn, I give up," she finally muttered.

His smile melted her into a quivering puddle. Heat shot through her veins, pooled in her stomach, and spread lower. Her dazed gaze remained on his face until he disentangled himself with an easy flick of his wrist, hinting at an intimate acquaintance with women's underwear. As he handed her the bra, his fingers brushed against hers. She could have sworn her skin tingled from the shock.

Her humiliation complete, she murmured, "Thank you," and prayed he'd leave. He didn't.

"Here, let me help." He began to gather up other bits of satin and lace.

"Thank you," she repeated, "but I can get the rest myself." Go away, go away, go away, she chanted silently, adding an emphatic expletive.

He ignored her, picking up a minuscule pair of hot-pink panties, a peach-colored lace nightgown, and another bra that should have been banned as an incitement to riot. The scents of satin and rose-petaled sin intensified in the air, assaulting her senses and firing images of those dexterous fingers dancing over—

Ruthlessly squelching her wayward thoughts, Gabrielle gritted her teeth, gathered the remainder to her bosom, and rose at the same time he did. Cheeks flaming, her chin angled in challenge, she thrust out an imperious hand.

"You have excellent taste," he told her, placing a few of the items in her outstretched hand. "No, that's mine," he added when she tried to take a silky black teddy from him.

"It doesn't look like your size," she snapped before she could help it.

He laughed, more heartily than she thought the comment deserved. "It's for a friend," he said, his voice rich with enjoyment. Another knee-weakening smile tugged at his lips.

Friend? Right. "So are these," Gabrielle said with an ironic smile.

He walked to the checkout counter with her, politely waiting his turn as she laid her things out. Rhonda, the clerk, greeted Gabrielle by name and asked if she'd received the latest sale circular.

"Haven't seen you in a month of Sundays," Rhonda continued, chatting as she rang up the sale. "Where you been hidin' yourself, honey?"

Her face heating anew, Gabrielle mumbled, "Work, mostly. I haven't had much time for shopping lately." She glared at the man, daring him to comment. His lips quivered, but he remained silent.

Spreading out powder-blue and white scented tissue paper, Rhonda wrapped each individual piece of lingerie with the care a jeweler gave to a perfect gemstone. "Oh, for God's sake, Rhonda, just put the damn things in a bag," Gabrielle finally said, her patience snapping like the last link in a trace chain.

She heard a choked-off laugh and turned her head, slicing the blond god with a razored glance. Rhonda grinned knowingly as she finished and handed her the striped paper shopping bag. Lighten up, Gabrielle, she told herself. You'll never see him again.

And a good thing too. He was obviously involved with someone. Even if he hadn't been, her performance had to be the Kodak moment of embarrassing incidents. She should be glad she'd never see him again.

Unable to resist a last glance, she looked over

her shoulder at him as she left. Their eyes met. He gave her another one of his bone-melting smiles and winked.

She *should* be glad . . . but she wasn't.

Gabrielle made it to the weekly meeting of the criminal defense litigation section with minutes to spare. She took a seat at the huge conference table, sinking into the chair beside Nina Abbot, a junior attorney she'd struck up a friendship with and who often assisted Gabrielle with her caseload. Nina didn't stand on ceremony with Gabrielle, and Gabrielle liked it that way. There was already too much pomp and circumstance at CG&S.

"Okay, let's hear the rest of it," Gabrielle said, referring to a conversation she and Nina had begun earlier that day.

"Surely you've seen him," Nina said. "He transferred here weeks ago. Where have you been, girl? What have you been doing?"

Gabrielle figured she was the only person in the Dallas office who hadn't yet met Devlin Sinclair. The hotshot defense attorney who'd just transferred from the Houston branch was rumored to have come to Dallas at a senior partner's urging. She knew Sinclair's reputation, of course, just as she knew the reputations of all of the competitive defense attorneys within the large firm. However, since the firm maintained offices all over the

Southwest, she had never met the majority of them.

"I've been buried under the legal avalanche of the century, remember?" she said to Nina. "I didn't think I'd ever wade through the paperwork. Besides, I know you. You think any male between the ages of twenty-five and sixty has potential."

"Not just potential." Nina shook her head and sighed. "No, this guy is absolutely—Oh, God, there he is." She brushed her blond bangs away from her face and patted at the cascade of curls falling to her shoulders. "He's coming over here. Maybe my horoscope was right, maybe—Gabrielle." This was accompanied by an elbow digging sharply into Gabrielle's ribs. "He's staring at you."

Smiling at her friend's sotto-voce discourse, Gabrielle turned her head. *No. Tell me no*, she thought, her blood congealing as she watched a man walk toward her with a swift, confident stride. Blond hair. Gray eyes. A long, lean, cool drink of water. Heaven help her, she needed a drink.

"You bum!" Nina whispered in her ear. "You have met him. How could you not tell me?"

He stood before her smiling, a heart attack just waiting to happen. "Devlin Sinclair." He held out his hand. "I don't believe we've been formally introduced."

Gabrielle extended a limp hand and said faintly, "Gabrielle Rousseau." She could only thank God that her mouth hadn't dropped open.

Taking the chair beside her, he said, "Rousseau? The McDermott case, right? Heard about that this morning." He looked at her with approval—and not a trace of jealousy. "Congratulations. Tough case."

Get a grip, you fool, she lectured herself. *You face rabid DA's daily. Take control here.*

"Thank you," she said.

Brilliant response, Counselor.

There wasn't time for more, thank heavens. Just then the section chief, Sid Norris, entered, and the meeting began.

An hour later, Gabrielle felt much better. Terminal boredom had helped settle her nerves. Sid had actually complimented her on the McDermott case, an act that was unheard of for the chief attorney.

She risked a surreptitious glance at Devlin Sinclair. So what if he thought of her as that klutz who'd fallen at his feet in the Midnight and Lace lingerie shop? She consoled herself with the certainty that he'd remember her courtroom victories a lot longer than her clumsiness. Her successes were the bottom line.

The meeting over, Sid called out to her as she started to leave the room. "Rousseau, I want to see you in my office. A private matter. It won't take long."

Gabrielle groaned silently. Sid's "not long" could mean anywhere from ten minutes to two hours, not including the time spent waiting for him to appear. Gathering her papers, she exchanged a wry glance with Nina before she left the room.

The familiar sizzle of ambition hit her the moment she stepped inside Sid's office. Settling comfortably into a leather side chair and closing her eyes, she let her imagination take wing. The siren call of achievement beckoned her. Partner. What a seductive sound the word made, even if only spoken in her mind. It meant dark, gleaming tones of a richly polished mahogany desk. Clear, sparkling crystal water goblets. A staff of people to do the drudge work, her own parking space instead of the half-mile hike in the Texas heat or freezing drizzle. A beautifully appointed, spacious office instead of the dreary cracker box she now inhabited. The scent of cool leather surrounded her in a cushion of hopeful affluence, success in shades of burgundy.

Success would mean that she'd been right to leave her past behind. Failure would mean she might as well have stayed where she was . . . stayed *who* she was.

Another scent tugged at her senses, growing stronger as the seconds stretched by. A heady, masculine scent of . . . power.

"I seem to be interrupting. Again." The deep male voice came from the doorway of Sid's office.

Already, she knew that voice. Its smoky bass tone made her think of sex and midnight sin. Gabrielle opened her eyes and gazed at Devlin Sinclair. The man had no right to look that good. Or to look so totally at ease. So . . . right, dammit. As if the office were his, instead of his boss's. His success rate was, in her opinion, advantage enough.

"This is a private meeting, Sinclair. I'll tell Sid you're looking for him."

"He knows," Sinclair said, stepping inside and crossing to the window. "He told me to meet him here. Something about a confidential matter. I assume he wants to see both of us. Some view," he added admiringly, looking out at the Dallas skyline. "You lived here long?"

See them both? "Why?" Gabrielle demanded, rising and striding to the window to stand beside him.

Sinclair's eyebrows lifted as he turned to look at her. "Curiosity. Your accent isn't from these parts."

What the devil did her accent have to do with anything? she wondered before she realized they were talking about two different things. "Not that," she said impatiently. "Why did Sid ask you to meet with him privately?"

His lips quirked, nearly a smile. "I have no idea. Do you?"

She didn't, dammit. And she didn't like it. Gabrielle had never liked surprises, even as a child. Not since she was six years old and her mother died unexpectedly. It would be just like Sid to have brought Devlin Sinclair to Dallas expressly to ruin her chances of advancement. Sid, the chauvinistic creep, couldn't stand the fact that Gabrielle—a mere female—had the best record and billed the most hours in their section. Considering her reputation, Sid couldn't afford to ignore her, but he loved seeing her nose bent out of joint. And if the rumors were true and Sid was really thinking of retiring . . . Voilà, Devlin Sinclair. Sid's replacement?

Over her dead body!

"You have very expressive eyes," he said, with that damnable smile tickling at his mouth. "You're glaring at me like you'd like to spit roast me over a slow fire. Why is that? I didn't put that display in the middle of the walkway, you know."

"I knew it! I knew you'd bring that up." Her forefinger jabbed him in the chest, squarely in the middle of the geometric design adorning his silk tie. "Listen, Sinclair, just because we met in a lingerie shop—" Abruptly, she halted, removing her finger from his chest. None of this was his fault. Maybe. She didn't trust him, though. Not one inch. She suspected his ambitions were on par with hers or he'd never have reached his current level in the firm's hierarchy.

"Absolutely right," he agreed, nodding. "A beautiful woman should feel no need to apologize for buying expensive lingerie."

Her eyes narrowed. In her experience flattery hid ulterior motives. She crossed her arms over her chest and strove not to stamp her foot. "I'm not apologizing. And I'm not beautiful. Don't try that line with me."

He put a finger under her chin and tilted her

head up. Examining her solemnly, he said, "No, I suppose not. Not classically beautiful, anyway. Your mouth is too wide, for one thing. And your nose turns up. But beauty is subjective. Your face is unusual. I like it."

She knew how he won over juries, or at least the women jurors. He hypnotized them with his eyes and that damnably deep, sexy voice. His almost smile was the clincher. Well, she was too shrewd to fall for Counselor Smooth. "I'm so thrilled," she said through her teeth, "that my face meets with your approval, Mr. Sinclair. You can't imagine what that means to me."

He laughed and dropped his hand just as Sid Norris entered the office. Sid's beady-eyed gaze scrutinized her for a second longer than his usual dismissive glances. Gabrielle damned the flush Sinclair's touch had provoked. Lord only knew what Sid was imagining.

Her own imagination had started working overtime the moment she saw Devlin Sinclair. And the fact that she'd met him in a lingerie shop, for heaven's sake, didn't help matters any. Lord, why did he have to look, not to mention sound, like every woman's fantasy?

Hold it right there, she told herself, cutting off the thoughts. Tripping over that display had scrambled her mind as well as bruised her dignity.

"Have a seat," Sid said, looking them both over with what Gabrielle thought of as his ferret-faced expression. "I'll get right to it. I've just been handed a case that I'd ordinarily take care of myself. However, my current commitments won't allow me to devote the time and attention needed. So the two of you are going to take it on."

Sid paused and let that hang in the air, playing for maximum effect. Pregnant pauses were one of his specialties, and his pompous air never failed to irritate Gabrielle. This time there was an underlying note of challenge to his words as well. What was Sid up to?

"What case is this, Norris?" Sinclair asked.

"A high profile one." Sid picked up his half-glasses and propped them on his nose. "So it won't be easy, needless to say. You'll need to pull in some more help along with your regular teams. I don't care who you use, just make sure they can keep their mouths shut."

Why the emphasis on keeping quiet? Gabrielle wondered, gazing at her boss. Anybody too mouthy didn't last long at CG&S. Just what kind of case was he dumping on them? She couldn't believe he was pairing her up with Sinclair, but for a chance at promotion she'd work with the devil himself. Glancing at her soon-to-be partner, she thought she just might be doing that. After all, they called him Devil Sinclair. His courtroom reputation was as good as hers. Or better.

Though he looked prune-faced as ever, she knew Sid was enjoying his power. After another lengthy pause, he added, "Did I mention this case is important? Winning is a priority. Do anything necessary to achieve that. Anything at all. We can't afford to let this one go down."

Give me a break, Sid. Can you get any more melodramatic? she thought, grimacing. Who in the world was this client that rated two top trial lawyers? They'd probably be working on this case from dawn to well past midnight, six days a week.

"Has the client been charged?" Sinclair asked.

"Yes. In fact, you need to get bail set as soon as possible." Sid tapped his finger on the file on his desk and continued, "The charge is racketeering—protection extortion. Also gambling, running an illegal operation. Bail will likely be sky-high, but that won't matter. Just get him out as quickly as you can."

"Racketeering and gambling?" Gabrielle repeated. "What is he, some kind of organized crime lord?"

Sid's sour smile said it all. "As organized as it gets. Mafia."

Mafia. The word steamrolled through Gabrielle's mind as a double load of cinder blocks fell on her chest. "Who is the client?" Her heart beginning to race, her breathing shallow and fast, she waited. The Mafia was everywhere. Coincidence, she told herself desperately. No reason to panic.

"The feds think the Mafia is trying to set up a whole new operation here in Dallas. First I've heard of it, but that's what they're saying. If this man falls, so do a lot of others. The feds want the dons, so they busted Franco Sabatino, hoping he'll talk. I doubt the charges are trumped up. Make damned sure no one knows what your defense will be. You two are in for a hell of a fight. But winning will be one hell of a victory."

Blood roared in Gabrielle's ears, drowning out anything else Sid said. Her stomach churned with violent nausea. Her skin turned clammy and hot at once.

Franco Sabatino. The case that could make her career.

The man who could ruin it.

TWO

A silence fell in the office as Norris paused for breath.

Devlin rose to look out the window and give himself a moment to think. Why a Mafia client? As far as he knew, CG&S didn't ordinarily represent organized crime. His branch hadn't, anyway, but maybe the Dallas branch was different.

A hell of a victory, he thought. But what if they lost? He turned back to Norris. "Why are we taking on a Mafia case? Wouldn't they prefer to have one of their usual attorneys handle it?"

Norris leaned back in his chair, giving Devlin a hard look. "Obviously not or we wouldn't have the client. They want CG and S, they get us." Case closed, he looked at the file on his desk. "I trust neither of you will turn it down." He didn't bother to make it a question.

Like they had a choice, Devlin thought. It

couldn't have been clearer if Norris had held up a sign saying: "Take the case or forget a promotion." Norris had lured him to Dallas with promises of career advancement opportunities, among other things, but this wasn't the kind of case he'd had in mind when he'd agreed to transfer.

One Mafia client per career was enough for Devlin. His first private practice client, just after he left the public defender's office, had been Mafia. Luckily, Devlin had won the case. He knew other defense attorneys not as fortunate.

Devlin glanced at Gabrielle, wondering at her silence. Her eyes were closed, her face chalky white. Beads of sweat dotted her forehead. Afraid she was about to pitch forward and crack her head on Norris's desk, he crossed the room and braced a hand on her shoulder. "Are you all right?"

Her eyes fluttered open. She stared at him with a stunned expression. "Indigestion," she mumbled, lowering her gaze and pressing a hand to her chest. She waved him away. "Give me a minute."

He ignored that and stood beside her until he was certain she wouldn't faint. He'd never seen a vulnerable shark before, but with her head bowed and her dark brown hair nestled in a neat, professional twist at the nape of her neck, that was how Gabrielle Rousseau looked. The urge to comfort, to protect was strong—and annoying. After her color seeped back, he left her long enough to pour her a glass of water.

Norris's eyes had widened with alarm. "You're not coming down with the flu, are you?"

She shook her head, but didn't speak. After sipping some water, she took the handkerchief Devlin passed her to dab at the fine film of sweat on her forehead. "It's not the flu," she finally responded in a firmer voice. "I told you, it was just a touch of indigestion. I'm fine now."

Looking poised for flight, the chief attorney stared at her. Could be those rumors of Norris's ill health were true, Devlin thought. His skin carried a waxy pallor beneath the obligatory golfer's tan, and his face was drawn, as though he were in pain. Added to that, his determination to bring Devlin to Dallas made him almost certain Norris was planning early retirement and looking for a replacement.

Devlin Sinclair, Partner, had a nice ring to it. So did chief attorney of criminal defense litigation, for that matter.

He had a hunch that Gabrielle Rousseau thought those titles would sound better after her name. Judging by her courtroom success rate, she should be a worthy rival. Good, he liked a tough fight. As long as he ended up winning.

Finally, Norris nodded, apparently satisfied with Gabrielle's explanation. "Good." He rose, indicating the meeting was over.

Devlin kept an eye on Gabrielle as she got up from her chair and walked to the door of the office.

Her hand shook a little when she smoothed back her hair, but she seemed steady enough on her feet.

Norris picked up the file and tapped it against his palm. "I'll leave the matter in your hands then. Go see Sabatino." With that, he handed Devlin the file and practically shoved them out the door.

"I'm indebted to you," Devlin told Gabrielle as they started down the hall toward the elevators. "Next time he gets too long-winded I'll start the coughing."

For a moment she stared at him, then smiled wanly. "Sid has a bit of a phobia about germs in the workplace."

"Think he sprayed Lysol around after we left?" Devlin asked, hoping to drag a real smile out of her. She kept walking without responding. Apparently she didn't have much of a sense of humor.

Changing the subject, he said, "You don't seem too happy with our new client. Or is it me you're not too pleased with?"

She halted outside the elevator door and jammed a finger on the up button before turning to look at him. "Frankly, neither one."

Whatever had been wrong with her, he decided, she'd managed to pull herself together quickly enough after they stepped out of Norris's office.

Tucking the file under his arm, Devlin stuffed his hands in his pockets and let his gaze linger on her face. Man, she had some beautiful eyes. Right now they flashed like murder in shades of green. "I can understand Sabatino," he said. "I'm not happy about a Mafia case, either. But what have you got against me?" He offered her his most charming smile, the one that had melted more than one heart. "I'm basically civilized, and I've had all my shots."

"Civilized is hardly the word I'd use. Not with your courtroom reputation."

So . . . she knew his track record. Which meant she considered him a threat. And so he was, if her desire for advancement matched his. Pleased that she thought of him as dangerous, he grinned at her. "But that's in court." The elevator doors slid open, and he followed her inside. "Outside of court I'm as tame as a tabby cat."

After a derisive glance, she ignored him and stared straight ahead, affording him an appealing view of her profile. Why was she so prickly? Because they were rivals? Or maybe, he thought, because she was embarrassed about falling at his feet with a load of lingerie flimsy enough to stir a dead man's blood. Since Devlin wasn't anywhere close to dead, his libido stirred just thinking about it.

Who'd have guessed that the Queen of Sharks harbored a secret addiction to expensive lingerie? Sexy, expensive lingerie. An interesting insight into her personality, that little incident. And doubtless something she'd rather he didn't know about her.

Devlin followed her into her office, taking one of the chairs in front of her desk. Gabrielle didn't sit. Instead, she stalked the floor with a restless energy. Odd, he thought, how five minutes before she'd been close to fainting and there she was circling the room like a shark scenting blood.

He flipped open the file and glanced at the entries. "Let's get started here. What do you know about Sabatino?" he asked, leafing quickly through the pages.

"Nothing," she snapped, halting and glaring at him. Resuming her pacing, she added, "And I don't want to know anything, either."

His sharp glance went unnoticed. "Yeah, I try to steer clear of Mafia too. Looks like we're both in trouble this time. Funny, I thought CG and S normally avoided organized crime clients. Got any ideas why they didn't on this one?"

"No," she said flatly. "What's in the file?"

Okay, she didn't want to speculate yet. Why not? She was bound to have as much curiosity as he did about Norris's turnaround.

Unless she knew something he didn't. He studied her for a moment, noting her quick, jerky actions, the nervous energy that simmered under her skin. Was it just his suspicious mind or were her reactions a little out of kilter? He decided not to drop it just yet.

"You're bound to have some idea. You know Norris better than I do. Why would he—?"

Gabrielle interrupted, exasperated. "Did you ever consider that Sid's arm is being twisted? We're talking Mafia here."

True, he thought. It could be as simple as that.

"You've got a point." Dropping his gaze back to the folder, he said, "All the same, Norris didn't do us a favor on this one. Sabatino's no stranger to the system. He's been charged twice before. Prostitution and gambling rings. Nothing stuck. Charges were dismissed, once because the arresting officer screwed up and the second time the case was thrown out because of lack of evidence. Both arrests took place in New York." He looked up to gauge her reaction. "Wonder why he decided to move to Texas."

"Greener pastures," Gabrielle said, finally sitting. Eyes narrowing, she drummed a pen on her desk.

She was about to jump out of her skin with nerves, Devlin thought. He wondered if that was normal for her. "Could be. Or maybe he had a falling-out with his boss, Vito Donati. We'll know more after we talk to him. Are you ready to go to the jail? See what Sabatino has to say for himself."

"There's no need for us both to go," she said.

Devlin lifted an eyebrow and stared at her. "Do you want me to handle it alone?"

"No! I mean, why don't you let me handle it? You see what you can do about the hearing."

Dream on, sweetheart, he thought. He wasn't handing this case over to her or anyone else. Not when it could gain either of them a partnership, or at the very least, a stronger position. "Better both see him first. He's liable to get huffy when he realizes we aren't both there. Makes clients feel important to have more than one lawyer."

"Suit yourself," she said, shrugging. "I thought it might save time."

Save time, his butt. He noticed the way the muscles in her jaw tightened. She didn't want him seeing Sabatino. Obviously, she wanted the case herself. Not two minutes ago she said she didn't know or want to know anything about the Mafia, yet here she was trying to see Sabatino alone.

He stood up. "Speaking of time, we'd better get over to the jail. Your car or mine?" he asked, smiling. Having learned the power of his smile early on, Devlin wasn't above using it to charm a woman out of her secrets . . . or whatever else got between them.

"Both," Gabrielle said, grabbing her keys. "See you at the jail, Sinclair."

He shook his head ruefully, watching her leave. She didn't seem to have any use for his fabled charms.

Gabrielle drove to the jail on autopilot, thankful that the traffic was only mildly hideous. She wished she had the luxury of falling apart, but she didn't have time—not with that sharp-eyed piranha watching her every move. She had better tread carefully around Devlin Sinclair. Dammit, she felt like a bug trapped in a glass jar. How much had she given away in Sid's office with her unguarded reaction? Thank God, she hadn't fainted.

Franco Sabatino. Her hands tightened on the steering wheel. Why did he have to show up now, when her career was taking off? Fourteen years without a sound from him and now . . .

Calm down and think, she told herself. Franco couldn't have singled out CG&S by accident. He had to know it was the law firm she practiced with. Of course he did.

Forgetting caution as usual, she scraped the bottom of her Dodge Stealth when she pulled into the parking lot across from the jail. That stupid dip at the lot's entrance had cost her more money than she liked to think about.

She took the only spot available, next to Sinclair's silver-gray Beamer. He was leaning against the car door, hands in his pockets and legs crossed at the ankles, blond hair glinting in the sun. No wonder they called him Devil. Only a fallen angel could look so mouthwateringly good in hundred-degree heat. A tingle of pure lust shot through her veins. Idiot, she thought. This guy was her hottest competition.

Oh, he was hot, all right. Irritated at the stab of unwelcome attraction, she slid out of her car and scowled at him.

"You're doing it again," he said, taking her arm and walking beside her.

"Doing what?" Did he think she was going to fall down in the parking lot? She tried to remember the last time a man had treated her so courteously. If his manners hadn't seemed so natural to him, she would have been more suspicious of his motives.

"Glaring at me," he answered. "You're about to give me a complex."

"I doubt that," she said, but she felt a twinge of guilt. Didn't the man have any faults? He was supposed to be a piranha in the courtroom. Who would've thought he'd be so damned polite?

Smart. Sexy. Good-looking. His hand rested lightly, even respectfully, underneath her arm. Why was her skin tingling? What was it about this guy?

Well, for starters, she thought, he was gorgeous. She glanced up at him and, seeing his smile, wished she hadn't. Talk about a dangerous attraction. He was the last person she needed stirring her up. Even if he weren't her prime rival, she wasn't his type. Leggy Miller beer models were more likely his taste. Probably had one waiting for him now—wearing a slinky black teddy.

But did he have to be so . . . sexy?

Forget that, Gabrielle, she told herself. Your career is hanging by a thread. Pay attention to saving your butt instead of indulging your suddenly overactive libido.

Seated at the scarred rectangular table of the police station conference room, Gabrielle studied

Sabatino's file. Beside her, Devlin studied Gabrielle. A woman of contradictions, or at the least, many adverse layers. He hadn't quite pegged her yet, and he was good at that. Contradictions, he knew, usually had reasons behind them. Her odd behavior at the office would bear further examination.

The door opened to admit Sabatino, striding in with a sublime disregard for his jailer. Devlin rose and thanked the police escort before turning to Sabatino. "I'm Devlin Sinclair and this is Gabrielle Rousseau. We're your attorneys from Christian, Gilmer and Simmons."

Sabatino ignored him, staring at Gabrielle instead. "*Bellisima*," he said in flawless Italian. His mouth curved into a slow smile, not quite a leer. "Rousseau," he added musingly, his eyebrows lifting. "Tell me, *signorina*, have we met before?"

"Not that I remember," she said, her eyes flashing a warning Devlin could read as well as Sabatino. "And I have an excellent memory."

She made it sound like a threat. Intrigued, Devlin watched both of them. Though pale again, Gabrielle didn't look as bad as she had in Norris's office.

Shrugging her statement aside, Sabatino spoke to Devlin. "About time you got your asses over here." He took one of the rickety chairs and pulled it out to sit. "I've been in this stinking hole twelve hours already. When the hell are you getting me out?"

Some things never change, Devlin thought. Exactly the attitude he'd expected. "*If* we get you out," he said calmly. If Sabatino thought to intimidate him, he could think again. "The judge might not be inclined to grant you bail. Even if he does, it's going to be high, given the charges against you. Racketeering isn't a penny-ante crime, not on the scale you're into."

"Your job is to get my butt out, not to lecture me, pretty boy."

Devlin quelled an urge to wipe the sneer off Sabatino's mouth with his fist. "Call it what you want. Those are the facts."

"What about you, *cara*?" he said, turning to Gabrielle. "Are you going to lecture me?"

"I'm your lawyer, Sabatino," Gabrielle said flatly. "You can call me Ms. Rousseau or Gabrielle, but that's as close as we get. You'll be out in forty-eight hours, with a little luck."

"I thought CG and S was supposed to be good." His eyes narrowed, darkened. "That's too long. I want out today."

"Good is one thing. Miracles are another." Devlin added a rider to pacify him a bit. "But we'll try to expedite your bail hearing. Have you considered cooperating with the FBI?"

Sabatino made a crude gesture expressing his opinion of that idea. "*Omertà*," he said simply.

"A code of silence won't get your butt out of a sling, Sabatino," Devlin said. "You should think about it."

"It won't get me killed, either. Besides, I'm innocent. The cops set me up. Entrapment."

"You want to plead not guilty?" Gabrielle asked, her tone implying she didn't believe his innocence for a minute.

"*Sì, signorina.* And you will defend me?" he asked with a suave smile.

"We haven't decided yet which one of us will present your case," Gabrielle snapped.

What was going on between these two? Devlin wondered. Sabatino was obviously jerking her chain, but still . . . A little too much tension for them to be the strangers they portrayed themselves to be.

He could see Gabrielle's fingers gripped tightly around her pen. Her control wasn't come by easily. Maybe it was the simple fact that she didn't like the Mafia. Or it might be she just didn't like Sabatino's oily style. Devlin couldn't blame her for that. Come to think of it, he'd had about as much of Sabatino as he could tolerate in one sitting. They had all the information they needed for now.

"We'll notify you as soon as the bail hearing is set," he said, rising and going to the door to signal Sabatino's escort to come for him.

"Send the *signorina* instead of you next time," Sabatino suggested with a final significant glance at Gabrielle. Neither of them answered as the jailer led him away.

"Not a chance, turkey," Devlin muttered. He

turned to Gabrielle. "Looks like you've got an admirer."

She lifted a shoulder. "He'll get over it."

Yeah, but would she? She was upset, Devlin mused, though doing a good job of hiding it. "Are you ready to leave?"

"No, you go ahead." She hesitated. "There's another matter I should check on while I'm here."

"All right. I'll see you later, then. Looks like it's going to be a working dinner for us tonight. You want me to bring takeout?"

"Dinner?" she repeated blankly.

"Yeah, I figure we might as well eat. We need to discuss the bail hearing, talk about preliminary strategy. The client's a little antsy, not much interested in giving us breathing time. So? Your place or mine?" he asked on a lighter note.

"Oh." She rubbed a hand over her forehead, clearly distracted. "My place, I guess. 4123 Greenbriar. It's the pale yellow brick."

"Got it. I'll be there around seven."

"Fine." She waved at him absently and walked off in the opposite direction from the exit.

Now that, Devlin thought, watching her, had been a very strange meeting. Lots of hidden undercurrents and he wanted to know why. He was a patient man, though. If there was something between Gabrielle and Sabatino, he'd find out what it was. Eventually.

❖————————❖

Gabrielle waited until she was certain Sinclair had left, even going to the extent of checking the parking lot for his car, before she asked to see Sabatino again. If Sinclair found out . . . but she'd take that risk. She had to see Franco.

Though surprised, the jailer gave her no trouble about bringing Sabatino back to the conference room. A few minutes later, she and Franco sat on opposite sides of the table, measuring each other silently.

Go for the jugular, Gabrielle thought. "So, Franco, what rock have you slithered out from under this time?"

"Ah, Gabriela. *Bellisima, squisita!* My heart stopped when I walked in that door and saw you. It's been too long, *cara mia.*"

"It hasn't been nearly long enough. Cut the crap and tell me why you called my firm." *You low-down piece of scum*, she added silently. Oh, he was the same Franco. But she wasn't the same girl he'd known. She was older. And smarter and stronger.

He spread his hands. "I should think that is obvious. I needed a lawyer. A good one."

"Naturally, you thought of me." She skimmed a disgusted gaze up and down his solid form. Dark, she thought. Hair, eyes, and soul. Years later, he still looked good, if you forgot he was a monster. "Me. A woman you haven't seen in fourteen years."

"You have a reputation." With a calculating smile, he relaxed in his chair.

"Yes, I do. And if you want me to get you out of here, you'll level with me."

"Gabriela." He opened his eyes wide in what she knew was feigned distress. "Can you possibly think I would betray—?"

Gabrielle tamped down a surge of nausea. "We both know what you're capable of. Save the hearts and violins for some other fool. Did you contact me on your own? Or was it Vito's idea?"

"Vito misses you. He's never been the same, never stopped grieving."

Even after all this time, even despite the bitter memories, sadness swelled in her soul when she thought of him. "Did Vito set this up? Did he send you to me, to my firm?"

Franco hesitated, then shook his head. Gabrielle said nothing for a long moment, then she leaned forward and spoke very quietly, deliberately. "Then we won't bring Vito into this. Do you understand? He's not to be mentioned. I cut my ties with Vito fourteen years ago and you know why."

"You must—"

Her voice was calm and deadly icy when she interrupted. "Don't cross me, Franco. Or you'll find out that Vito isn't the only Donati you need fear."

Seconds ticked by while their gazes locked. Finally, Franco glanced away. "You wrong me, *cara*. I won't expose you."

"Good." Thank God, she sounded cool, because inside she shook with nerves. It would be a major mistake to let Franco know just how much he'd gotten to her. "Now that we understand each other, I'll see what I can do to get you out of jail."

"Ciao, mi bellisima Gabriela."

"Gabrielle Rousseau. Remember it." She repeated it silently as she left, as if saying her name would make the truth impotent. It only mocked her, though. She knew what would happen if the truth ever came out.

Ruin.

THREE

After ringing the doorbell three times, Devlin decided Gabrielle must have been held up at the jail or had gone back to the office. The door jerked open just as he started to turn away. She didn't say anything, but stood in the doorway and stared at him.

Dark brown hair caught in a topknot with the ends sticking straight up, no lipstick, mascara smudged under gorgeous green eyes. The features were the same, but . . . Who the hell was this woman? What had happened to Ms. Buttoned-up Dressed-for-success Gabrielle Rousseau?

His gaze dropped from her face to a baggy white T-shirt with the logo of a man holding an alligator guitar. "We be jazzin'," it read. Bare feet, cutoffs, and legs longer than a country mile completed the picture.

And judging by her bewildered expression, she didn't have a clue why he was there.

"Hi. I brought Chinese." He held up a plastic carton and a paper sack. "Hope that's okay, but you didn't say what you wanted."

"What I . . ." Laying a hand aside her head, she continued to stare as her voice trailed off and her brow furrowed in bafflement.

"You forgot," he said, a little amused to find his pride bruised. "You're hard on the ego, did you know that?" Women didn't forget dates, even working dates, with Devlin. They might break them, but they didn't totally forget them. Gabrielle, apparently, had.

"You'll live. I can't imagine your ego suffering for long." She stepped aside to let him in, obviously having regained her poise.

"Is that a compliment or an insult?"

Her mouth curved upward. "Take it whichever way you want. But if it makes you feel better, I didn't forget. I just didn't realize what time it was."

He let that pass, but he knew she *hadn't* remembered their working dinner. It piqued his vanity, especially since he didn't think the sexual pull between them was all on his side. Yet even more than insulting him, her forgetfulness aroused his curiosity. An attorney with Gabrielle's reputation wouldn't forget something like the Sabatino case. Could she really be a space cadet? He seriously doubted it. More likely, she was playing some kind of game.

Stepping over a pair of tan pumps lying drunkenly beside the front door, he walked inside and glanced around. The dining room and living room were combined. Instead of a table in the dining area, a black baby grand piano filled the entire space. A book stood open on the music tray over the keyboard and a piece of sheet music lay on the bench with another on the floor beside it. Not for looks, he thought. Obviously, she played.

The rest of the room was an odd mixture of tastes, ranging from a gorgeous Oriental rug covering the hardwood floor, to a piece of modern metal sculpture standing in a corner, to a well-used sofa and easy chair that denied any claim to fashion.

On the coffee table a glass lay turned over beside an open bottle of wine. That could explain her spaciness, he thought, except it didn't look like more than a glassful was missing from the bottle. A small horse stood beside the low glass-topped table, wagging its tail and lapping at the pale gold liquid dripping steadily onto the expensive rug.

No, not a horse. A large, ugly brown and black curly-haired dog.

"Rocky! Stop that!" Gabrielle tugged on the dog's collar, but it ignored her and simply swiped at the wine until it was gone. With a plop, the dog sat, its pink tongue darting out to lick the last lingering drops from its snout. "You sot," she accused.

Devlin laughed. "What is he? Besides a lush?"

"A pain in the rear. And he's a she. Come on,"

she said, picking up the wine bottle and glass and starting out of the room. "We'll eat in the kitchen."

Great legs, Devlin thought as he and the dog followed her. Long, shapely—but he shouldn't be thinking about her legs, however fantastic they were. He needed to think about business. Law, not legs.

Trouble was, he kept getting distracted. From the moment she landed at his feet in the lingerie shop, Gabrielle had intrigued him. Satin and lace underneath an ultraconservative business suit. The more he learned about her, the more curious he grew. Normally, he didn't allow a woman to distract him. Gabrielle did it without even trying. He thought about that for a moment. Maybe she *was* trying. It was a unique approach, if so.

The dog went out the back door along with Gabrielle's admonition not to dig. "She ate my sprinkler system last week," she said by way of explanation. "Puppies."

"Puppy?" He took the wine bottle from her and set it on the kitchen table along with the food. "That's a puppy? You mean she'll get bigger?"

Her smile softened the angles of her face. "Not exactly, but she'll fill out. We had a rash of burglaries a few months ago, and I decided to get a dog. The people at the shelter said she'd be a great watchdog. I must have sucker written on my forehead. So far she's been worthless. She sleeps like the dead and barks at everything in sight."

"You don't look like a sucker to me."

"Only for certain things," she said.

He wondered what those were, besides animals. "Maybe she'll improve with age."

"I suppose there's always that hope." She sounded doubtful. "Do you want a glass of wine?" Opening a cupboard, she looked over her shoulder at him.

"Sure. Here, let me get it." He reached toward the top shelf at the same time she did. Their hands collided, and one of the glasses fell, shattering on the white tile floor.

"Damn." Surrounded by a field of glass shards, she grimaced as she surveyed the mess.

"Sorry."

She shrugged his apology aside. "It wasn't fine crystal. Just one step up from jelly jars."

"You'd better let me clean it up. You're barefoot."

"Don't be sill—"

He picked her up in midsentence and set her on the counter. Enjoying her startled gasp, he let his hands linger at her waist. Tension shimmered, stretched tightly between them as they stared at each other. Slowly, he became aware of the soft feel of her beneath his hands, of her scent, faintly sultry, luring him closer.

His gaze dropped to watch her tongue dart out and moisten her lips. Was it an unconscious gesture? He couldn't be certain, but it sure as hell tempted him.

He leaned closer, until their mouths were only a few inches apart, and purposely lowered his voice to an intimate level. "Where's your broom?"

"My . . ."

"Broom," he supplied, watching the dazed expression leave her face.

Her eyes flashed with a murderous gleam. "In the pantry."

He grinned and began to think seriously on the merits of seduction.

"So, we're clear on the initial division of the research," Devlin said some two hours later. He sifted through the papers spread out over the coffee table, sticking a few of them in his briefcase.

"Yes." Gabrielle picked up one of the heavy law books from the floor in front of the couch and thumbed through it. "I'll tell my team tomorrow to start checking out the eyewitnesses."

When they first sat down to work, Gabrielle had pulled out a pair of brown horn-rimmed glasses. With that action, all traces of a space cadet had disappeared. Devlin decided she used that airhead attitude to throw people off guard. It was an effective strategy and heightened his curiosity about what made her tick.

"Take a break," he suggested. "We've done everything we can for tonight."

"Talked me into it." She took off her glasses

and laid them on top of the papers on the coffee table, then groaned and rolled her shoulders.

Devlin stretched his arm across the back of the couch, brushing his fingers over the nape of her neck. "You're the jumpiest woman," he said at her start of surprise. "Are you always that way?"

"I'm not—" She shivered when his fingers found a tight muscle and squeezed gently. "Jumpy. What are you—Hmm?" She stretched like a cat as he massaged her neck. "Don't . . . I don't think you should do that."

He smiled and continued flexing his fingers into the soft skin of her neck and shoulders. If she were as indifferent to him as she pretended to be, she wouldn't sound so wary. "Relax. It's only a neck rub."

"Sinclair, this is a business meeting," she said, but she didn't move away. Her eyes drifted shut and her head bowed as she relaxed beneath the subtle pressure of his fingers.

"We're through for the night, remember?" The tension started to ebb from her muscles. His gaze lit on the piano, reminding him of a question he'd meant to ask her earlier. "What kind of music do you play?"

"Bach, Beethoven . . . Mozart." Her voice sounded dreamier. "Schubert, Handel . . ."

Classical. That suited her, he thought. He found the image of her playing the piano surprisingly erotic. Maybe it was the idea of her hands gliding over the keys. "Do you play other music, as well?"

"Some." She paused and added, "But I like classical best. It's the most . . . satisfying to me."

"Are you any good?"

She tilted her head up, shooting him a challenging look over her shoulder. "What do you think?"

He smiled and shifted closer, keeping his hands on her shoulders. "I think you wouldn't play if you weren't any good."

"Probably not," she said, and laughed softly. "When I was younger I wanted to be a concert pianist."

"What changed your mind?" She was almost fully relaxed now, and the feel of her smooth skin was tempting the hell out of him. He told his hands to stay put. "What made you choose law instead?"

Her shoulders tensed. "I grew up. It's hard to make a living as a pianist. Law seemed . . . safer."

Safer, he thought. An odd choice of words. "Do you ever regret it?" His hands skimmed down to her back, kneading as they talked.

"No. I still have my music. Only now I've got a law career as well." She was silent a moment. "That's not my neck."

"I know. Your back's tight too." She turned to face him. He slid his arm around her waist and eased her close, his hand resting on the small of her back.

"Forget it," she said, slapping a hand on his chest.

He bent his head, his mouth a heartbeat away from hers. "Why? It's just a kiss, Gabrielle. Perfectly . . . safe." He tugged the banana clip out of her hair and slipped his hand into the thick brown waves. Her eyes turned a deep jade green as alarm and another more carnal emotion filled them. Desire. He'd kissed enough women to recognize that look in her eyes.

He smiled. Let her deny the attraction now. It simmered between them and tingled in the air. There was no way he'd believe she didn't feel it too.

"That was a move tonight in the kitchen," she said. Her voice had turned husky; it rippled along his skin and lingered like a caress.

Slowly, he shook his head. "No, that wasn't a move." He smiled again, and his own voice deepened. "This is a move."

His mouth lowered until it just touched hers, sipping, nipping, cruising gently over her lips. He felt her surprise in the way she relaxed and opened for him. As he slipped his tongue inside, hers came out to touch his, tentatively at first and then growing bolder. She tasted faintly of wine and warm, giving flavors.

Devlin stroked his hand up her back and deepened the kiss. Her arms lifted to wrap around his neck. Bewitched by the soft pressure of her mouth, he forgot he'd had an objective in mind when he kissed her. A fist of need slammed hard into his belly as she heated to a blaze in his arms. He slid his tongue inside her mouth, withdrew, slid in again in a slow, primal rhythm. She moaned and wrapped herself up in him, answering the motions of his tongue with hers.

A tiny portion of his mind told him to back off, that this woman was dangerous. Then she nipped at his lower lip and pressed against him, her breasts crushed against his chest. She moaned again, a full, throaty sound that made him want to strip her out of her clothes and see what those long legs felt like wrapped around him.

Devlin tore his mouth from hers. If he hadn't, he'd have had her flat on her back in another thirty seconds. And while that had seemed like a great idea before he kissed her, he wasn't so sure now. A woman who went up in flames the minute he touched her and who blasted his self-control to smithereens with a kiss deserved to be handled with extreme caution.

She shoved hard at his chest. "Let go of me."

Her voice was shaky, which didn't gratify him as much as it might have, since he suspected his own voice might not be quite steady either. He released her and moved away, taking two mental steps backward as well. They stared at each other in silence.

It was just a kiss, he thought. What the hell was wrong with him? He felt like he'd been in a war zone. She looked like she had. Her mouth was red, her lips swollen from kissing him. He wanted, quite badly, to kiss her again.

"I don't get involved with my coworkers," she said.

"Okay. We won't get involved." Mindless, fantastic sex sounded good to him.

Her eyes narrowed. "I mean it. Don't kiss me again."

Regaining some of his accustomed cool, he smiled at her. "Gabrielle, you know as well as I do that I'm going to do a lot more than kiss you." His smile broadened. "But not tonight."

She looked like she wanted to throw something at him. "You'd better have your back checked out, Counselor. Even the strongest will break under a two-ton load of ego."

Ego, was it? He didn't think so. "That kiss wasn't all on one side."

"Go away," she said through gritted teeth. "Far away."

"For now, I will." But he'd be back. When he'd figured out how she blew his cool so easily.

She pointed at the door. He gathered his papers together and stuffed them in his briefcase, holding her gaze as he did so. He'd proved one thing anyway. She sure as hell wasn't indifferent to him.

Devlin picked up his briefcase and strolled out, pausing in the doorway to give her a last wicked grin. "See you in court, Counselor."

She barely missed his fingers when she slammed the door shut.

You are a fool, Gabrielle told herself as she sank onto the couch after Devlin left. What in Hades was the matter with her? Her life was one step away from blowing up in her face. Her arch rival was now her partner in the case that could wreck her career. One whisper of her past and Devlin Sinclair would use her back as a stepping stone in his quest for a partnership.

And what was she doing? she asked herself, viciously gathering her papers and slapping them into a pile. Trying to find a way out of the tightest spot she'd ever been in? Applying all her energies, her logical, legally trained, supposedly bright mind to saving her endangered butt?

No, she was thinking about sex. Hot, mind-blowing sex. With Devlin Sinclair.

She had to be crazy. First of all, she barely knew him. And she wasn't the type to flip over a pretty face. She'd learned that lesson well years before. Tonight, though, she'd reached a new level of insanity. The fact that she hadn't been involved with a man in a long time was no excuse for her stupidity.

Still, it was just a kiss. No reason for her to turn herself inside out, even if it had been an incredible kiss. She would simply be very careful that he didn't touch her again. Then this . . . urge would die a natural death. She hoped.

Gabrielle consoled herself with the knowledge that tonight she'd been especially vulnerable. Her weakness had allowed a simple chemistry to get out of hand, to take on more importance than it merited. Two glasses of wine were enough to lower her guard. Added to that, she'd been in the midst of a flood of memories when she'd answered the door to him. That smooth, good-looking devil had been a welcome diversion from memories she didn't want to face.

Memories, she thought. Franco. She had to decide what to do about him. Damn the man, why did he have to show up now, after all these years of blessed peace? One word from him and her career was history. No reputable firm would have her if they knew the truth about her past.

Was Franco only after a good lawyer, like he'd said? Surely to God he didn't still want . . . her. The idea made her skin crawl. Shuddering, she tried to push Franco's image from her mind, but the trap of memories yawned open its gaping jaws. Fourteen years later she could still hear the voices. Past and present merged as she relived the scene in her mind.

"Your lover is gone," Franco had told her. "Ten thousand dollars. He could have gotten more, you know, but then I never thought your Ben was very bright."

Money? she'd thought. He was saying Ben had

taken a bribe? The blood drained from her face. "No. Ben loves me, I know he does. He wouldn't do that." But her heart beat double-time in her throat, her stomach surged with nausea. What if Franco was right?

Franco's smug, evil smile said it all. "He took the money and ran. You're mine now. Accept it, *cara*. We'll be married in a few weeks."

"I'd rather be dead," she said, not knowing how close she would come to that exact thing.

And that last night, when Franco had come to her in rage . . . Gabrielle shook her head hard, trying to fling the shadows away. No, she didn't want to think of that. Couldn't allow herself to think of what had happened—and had nearly happened—that night. It was past and buried, and she would leave it there. She could deal with Franco Sabatino, as long as she didn't let the memories choke her.

She rose and walked to the piano. Dragging one finger across the keyboard, she wished she felt like playing. Sleep would be a long time coming. She could think about Franco and ruin or Devlin Sinclair and sex.

Sinclair won, hands down.

FOUR

Gabrielle took the steps leading to the courthouse two at a time. She hadn't dozed off until after four A.M. and consequently, she'd overslept that morning. Not good, considering she needed to be at court early for the bail hearing. Still, she made it with a few minutes to spare.

Judge Claiborne, the bail judge, had earned a reputation as a hardnose. With her luck, Gabrielle thought, he'd pick today to go soft. While keeping Franco in jail wouldn't solve her problem, it wouldn't hurt matters, either. But she had a feeling he'd make bail—and then what would she do?

As she strode down the long hallway leading to the courtroom, her heart started to pound. She ignored it and pressed on, but her heart rate increased rapidly, then her throat began to close up. Her steps slowed, and she halted, gasping, trying to breathe. Sweat started beading on her forehead.

No. Oh God, no, she thought, looking around frantically for a private room. It had been so long, she almost hadn't recognized the symptoms. Her heart pounding at the speed of sound, she tried to breathe in, but no air moved through her lungs. Why now when it hadn't happened to her in years?

"Gabrielle, wait up," she heard a voice call out from behind her.

The voice registered, barely, through the dizzying numbness. Devlin Sinclair.

Ignoring him, she spotted the women's rest room and rushed toward it. She prayed she'd get inside before he caught a glimpse of her pale, clammy face. Dashing in, she stumbled into one of the stalls. Seconds later, cursing silently, still gasping for breath, she emerged, grabbed some paper towels, and darted back inside the stall. Her fingers fumbled with the paper as she made a fist and shaped the paper towels around it. Then she bent over and put her head between her legs.

Breathe, she told herself, forcing air into the makeshift paper bag. *In and out, real slow. Calm down, you're okay. Just breathe.* She had no idea how much time passed when her gasping breaths finally slowed and her heart rate returned to normal. Gabrielle opened her eyes and sat up, still shaky, but grateful the attack was over. Lightheaded, she waited as spots swam in her vision, then cleared away. Thank God no one had come into the rest room. This wasn't a problem she wanted anyone else to know about.

If her colleagues knew—She closed her eyes again and groaned. God, wouldn't this be one for the gossip mill. Gabrielle Rousseau, so-called Queen of Sharks, reduced to panic attacks in the women's rest room. Sid Norris would eat it up like a kid with a candy bar.

And Sinclair, she thought, moaning. What would *he* make of it? He already knew more about the intimate details of her life than she'd ever have admitted voluntarily. Lingerie addiction, panic attacks . . . No, she didn't want him to know about this.

After giving herself a few more seconds, she went to the sink to splash cool water on her face and check her makeup for damage. Her face looked pinched, but otherwise fairly normal.

A panic attack. Not just a twinge of one, but a full-fledged, scary as hell humdinger of an attack. What was going on here? She'd overcome that particular problem years ago.

Gabrielle wiped her hand across her forehead, staring into the mirror unseeingly, remembering other times, other places. When she'd first started out in law, it had happened like clockwork. Every time before she stepped into a courtroom, she hyperventilated. After six months of carrying a paper bag in her purse and ducking into rest rooms before her court appearances, she'd finally gotten a grip on her weakness. It had taken a year or more before she felt confident enough to dispense with the bag totally. And she hadn't had a recurrence until now.

Until she had to step into a courtroom and defend Franco Sabatino.

"Morning," Devlin said to Gabrielle, falling into step alongside her on the way to the courtroom.

"Get your jollies by loitering outside women's rest rooms, Sinclair? I'd have thought you had better things to do."

Same sharp tongue as the day before, he thought. "Loitering's one of my favorite pastimes." She was every inch the successful attorney this morning, he noticed, his gaze taking in her dark suit and her hair coiled in a neat knot at her neck, not a strand escaping. A half smile pulled at his mouth. "Still mad at me about last night? Or are you always cranky in the morning?"

"There goes that ego again," she said. "Why would you, or for that matter, last night, have anything to do with my mood?"

Devlin studied her. One thing he knew already, Gabrielle wasn't always what she seemed. She looked calm, collected, together. Still, he thought, staring at her profile as they walked, he didn't doubt she'd been up half the night looking for loopholes, trying to figure a way to weaken or destroy the prosecution's case. Planning a strategy for the best way to spring Sabatino on bail.

"I think we'll leave the answer to that question for later," he finally said. "When we don't have a bail hearing."

Unresponsive, she stepped inside the courtroom when he held the door for her. Following her, he tried to get his mind back on the law and away from her reactions to him the night before—and even more importantly, away from *his* reactions to her. Devlin had never had a problem settling down to business. It annoyed him mightily that he was having a hard time of it now. And that he suspected the reason for that was his preoccupation with a certain lady lawyer. The sooner he established that he was the one in control, the better.

A short time later the bailiff led an unsubdued Sabatino in, leaving him standing between Devlin and Gabrielle. If Devlin hadn't been watching Gabrielle so closely, he might have missed her slight shiver as Franco greeted her with the word Devlin was already beginning to hate.

"*Bellisima,*" Sabatino said to her, seemingly unperturbed by the fact that odds were better than even that his bail would be denied. Devlin hadn't been joking when he'd told Franco that getting him bail would be no easy matter. And Claiborne, the bail judge, didn't much care for Mafia.

Gabrielle recovered herself quickly, shooting their client a murderous look, but otherwise ignoring him as they waited for the judge.

The tension between Sabatino and Gabrielle was so thick, Devlin couldn't have pierced it with a lance. Why was it there? It didn't make sense. It invited him to investigate just why those two couldn't be in the same room without throwing out sparks of electricity. And the sparks weren't sexual attraction, at least on Gabrielle's part. He'd bet a year's legal fees on that. Gabrielle didn't dislike Sabatino, she loathed him. Devlin intended to find out why.

"All rise," the bailiff said. And the hearing began.

Subtle and haunting, the strains of a Vivaldi violin concerto enhanced the classic ambience of The Riviera, one of Dallas's finest French restaurants. Chic, sleek, and ruinously expensive, the voluptuous blonde seated beside Devlin blended perfectly into her surroundings.

"Darling, you never did say why you keep breaking our dates. Or why you were so late tonight, for that matter," Angela said, her lovely mouth curving into a pout.

"No, I didn't, did I?" Devlin agreed. He'd spent the last three days working on the Sabatino case, but he saw no need to explain himself to Angela.

"I waited at the bar forever. I swear, I had half a mind to let that nice man"—she nodded at a gray-haired, distinguished-looking man a few tables away—"buy me a drink." She sent Devlin a reproachful glance.

Devlin's mouth lifted at one corner. "Why didn't you?"

Angela gave a surprised tinkle of laughter. "Are you saying it wouldn't have bothered you?"

"You're perfectly free to do what you want," he told her, and shrugged. "Don't let me stop you." Angela's recent surge of possessiveness was grating on his nerves. He didn't like being crowded, especially by a woman who wasn't even his lover. He tried to remember why he'd been so interested in Angela in the first place. Then she leaned forward, her neckline gaping open to expose her cleavage.

Now he remembered.

His gaze lifted to her face. Judging by Angela's superior smile, she interpreted his comment to mean that he would have been bothered to see her drinking with another man. Her ego was even healthier than his, he thought.

Conversation had never been one of Angela's most attractive qualities, and tonight was no exception. While she chattered, Devlin's thoughts drifted. The bail hearing the day before had gone better than he'd expected, and they'd gotten Sabatino out of jail with little difficulty. Replaying the hearing in his mind, he wondered again what exactly was going on between Gabrielle and Sabatino. Something was—he could feel it every time they were together. Neither one's reaction was, in his opinion, normal or reasonable. At least for two people who claimed not to know each other. How could he go about finding out?

Of course, he didn't know Gabrielle all that well, and his own reaction to her hadn't been entirely . . . reasonable. Unless you considered sudden, overwhelming lust reasonable. Pondering that, he frowned. He remembered her mouth and what it had felt like opening beneath his, the softness of her breasts crushed against his chest. Reason had very little to do with it, he decided.

Angela's hand massaged his thigh underneath the snowy white tablecloth, bringing his attention back to her. "Devlin." She purred his name and inched closer. Her other hand curved around her wineglass, caressing it as suggestively as she was his leg. "You're a million miles away. I bet I know what you're thinking about." A provocative smile played on her lips.

Staring at her, Devlin doubted it. A month ago he'd been intent on getting Angela into his bed, but lately . . . lately he wasn't sure she was worth the effort. He hadn't noticed before, or if he had, it hadn't bothered him, how hard and calculating her beautiful blue eyes were. She was gorgeous, but so predictable. Utterly, boringly predictable.

"You've been very patient with me," she went on. Her fingers walked higher up his leg. "I can't tell you how I appreciate that." Her hand inched ever upward. She murmured throatily, "Would you like to come to my place after dinner?"

Her place. Here it was, the invitation he'd been angling for. Now that she'd given it, why did the idea generate nothing but a faint boredom? Perhaps because he knew that to Angela he would merely be one more man in a procession of lovers who could gratify either her vanity, her pocketbook, or her social ambitions.

So what? he asked himself. It was a familiar game, and given her beauty, one he should have enjoyed. Yet he found himself wishing, for a brief, unguarded moment, that something else existed. That somewhere there was a woman who wanted the man he was and not the facade he presented. Devlin nearly laughed aloud, amused at a belief he hadn't held in over a decade, not since he was young and extremely naive about women and life.

As for Angela, he realized, it hadn't been a matter of patience. He'd simply lost interest. "Another time, sweetheart. I've got work waiting at the office." Her astounded expression made it hard not to laugh. Clearly chagrined, she punished him by remaining silent until the check arrived. Devlin counted it a blessing.

Though it had only been an excuse, Devlin decided to stop by the office after dropping Angela off. He figured he might as well salvage something from the evening. As he walked down the hallway, he noticed a faint gleam of light shining from beneath the door to the CG&S law library. He shoved the door open and halted on the threshold. Shadows filled most of the room, but a lamp illuminated one corner where Gabrielle sat, bent over a table covered with briefs. It was midnight, the room's silence broken only by the sound of pages turning. Obviously, she didn't win her cases by stinting on research. He wondered what that concentration would feel like directed at him.

"Working awfully late, aren't you, Counselor?" he asked, strolling into the room and coming to a halt beside her chair. Deep into her reading, she glanced up at him, her eyes behind the lenses of her glasses taking a moment to show recognition. What was it about those horn-rimmed glasses of hers that attracted him? The thought of taking them off?

Her gaze ran over him. "Hot date stand you up, Sinclair?" Her voice was soft and husky, as if she hadn't spoken in hours.

A bedroom voice, he thought, enjoying the sound of it. Grinning, he propped his rear against the edge of the table, his leg only a few inches from her hand. "Careful. Can't you tell you're speaking to a heartbroken man?"

She snorted, and her voice regained its customary sharp edge. "You don't have one to break."

"Why do you say that?" He edged closer, brushing his leg against her hand, pleased when she tensed but didn't move it away.

"A passing acquaintance with your ego."

He leaned over and traced a finger down her nose. He liked the way it tilted up at the end, and he liked even more hearing the telltale catch of her breath as she drew it in. "You're just ticked off because I won't pretend there's no attraction between us." She opened her mouth, no doubt to protest, but he continued on. "Speaking of hot," he said, rolling up his shirtsleeves, "what happened to the air conditioner? Is it broken again?"

She ground her teeth audibly before she answered him. "Sid turns it up at night and locks the thermostat. It doesn't bother him that those of us who work late swelter." Her elegant musician's fingers plucked at the neckline of the white silk blouse clinging damply to her chest. "Do you think I like sitting in the dark? The overhead lights made it unbearable in here."

Devlin had an idea that the heat wasn't totally due to the temperature of the room. A small bead of moisture trickled down her chest, disappearing in the shadowy valley between her breasts. He wondered what she'd taste like if he ran his tongue along that line. "I can think of several things to enjoy in the dark. Reading isn't one of them."

Abruptly, Gabrielle shoved her chair back and stood. "If you don't mind, I'm working." She stalked to the light switch and flipped on the overhead.

Blinking at the sudden, harsh glare, he grinned, knowing he'd gotten to her. "Yeah, that's why I came down here. Had an idea about Sabatino's case and wanted to look it up." He followed her over to the book stacks, standing behind her while she scanned the shelves. His hand covered hers as she reached for a book.

Glancing over her shoulder, she snapped, "Do you mind?"

"Not at all," he said politely, masking his smile as he pulled out the heavy leather-bound volume and handed it to her. Almost at random, he chose another and carried it to the table, switching off the overhead lights on his way. He settled comfortably into the seat across from hers. A frown tightened her mouth as she concentrated on her book.

Several minutes passed. When Devlin judged her to have relaxed her guard, he spoke. "Has Sabatino been hassling you?" A grunt was her only response. "I heard some rumors about him and one of his former lawyers. A woman."

At that she looked up, her expression one of distrust. "So?"

"He didn't like the way she handled his case, so he had her roughed up. No one could prove he did it, but she's convinced it was Sabatino."

Gabrielle didn't look surprised; rather, she looked amused and a little disgusted. "Nice try, but I'm not giving up the case."

"No one expects you to. That's not why I told you. I thought you should know the kind of client we're dealing with. Just as a precaution, that's all. But then"—he flipped a page leisurely—"you and Sabatino seem to have an understanding. Almost like you know each other. A kind of . . . rapport, I guess you'd call it." Smiling blandly, he raised his gaze to meet hers. Her face had paled. "Funny how that kind of thing happens, isn't it? Especially with two strangers."

Her eyes were like green chips of ice, standing out against the pallor of her skin. Her voice was as hard as her eyes. "I'm his lawyer. That's as far as our 'understanding' goes."

He cocked his head, considering her. "Sabatino would like it to be more than that."

"All this on the basis of a few meetings?" She grabbed at the hair falling in her face and tucked it back. "Get real. He just wants us to save his butt."

"Sure he does." Shutting his book, Devlin caught her gaze and held it. Her eyes were still hard, and even warier. "But he wants more than that." A pulse throbbed at her throat. Devlin realized he wanted to taste her there, too, to feel her heartbeat against his mouth, to run his lips over that soft, gleaming skin. Wanted it so much that it took him a moment to remember his strategy, to remember why he'd started this line of talk. "Sabatino wants you."

Fear flashed in her eyes before she lowered her gaze. Raw fear, more than the moment called for to Devlin's way of thinking. Enough fear to send her running?

"Assuming you're right," she said, her voice tight, "that's my problem, isn't it? If you think Franco's little games will make me roll over and give you this case, you're wrong."

Franco? Franco's little games, she'd said. Like she had more than a passing acquaintance with those games. Or with the man. "You know him, don't you?" Devlin asked softly.

Her expression shut down, lights off. "I know his type. And I know what you're trying to do. Forget it. I don't scare that easily."

But she was scared. Devlin sensed it, felt it in the tension pervading the room. Hell, he could almost smell it. Why? Why was she so frightened, yet so determined to continue with the case? "What makes you think I want you off the case?"

"Nothing except the little fact that you don't want to share the glory if we win. I know what you want."

He smiled at her, slow and easy. "Do you?" he murmured, his gaze lingering on her mouth.

Her eyes widened, then she looked away and began collecting her papers. He was reminded of how flustered she'd been when she dropped her lingerie and he helped her gather it up.

"It's late," she said. "I'm going home."

He waited until she finished, then rose and went to the door with her.

"What are you doing?" she asked him as he turned out the light and shut the door behind them.

"Walking you to your car."

She strode down the hall, halting at the elevator. Facing him, her chin lifted arrogantly, she said, "I'm a big girl, Sinclair. I can get to my car by myself."

Hands in his pockets, he relaxed, his shoulder against the wall. "You can also get mugged."

"I know self-defense. Besides, I moved my car to the lighted lot attached to the building. The security guard will watch out for me."

"Humor me. It's my Southern upbringing."

She threw her hand up. "Have it your way," she said, and stalked inside the elevator when the doors opened.

I intend to, he thought, following her in.

FIVE

As they stepped out of the elevator Devlin took her arm, just as he had every other time they'd walked together. Again, Gabrielle wondered if it was his upbringing that prompted him or if it was merely an excuse to touch her.

Their footsteps echoed hollowly in the deserted garage. Unable to resist, she glanced at him. His hair fell across his brow, a slash of gold in the gloom. His profile presented the chiseled perfection of one of Michelangelo's sculptures. A masterpiece of living, breathing man, not marble. Sleek, powerful, beautiful, a cougar ready to pounce the minute he found out the truth about her and Franco.

Devlin was much too astute to chatter. No, he'd let her mull over what he'd said in the library, and if that wasn't bad enough, his silence only intensified her awareness of his presence. Magnified the smell of him, the faint whiff of his aftershave and more, the male scent of power, and danger. What was wrong with her? Instead of finding ways to keep him in the dark, all she could think about was . . . sex.

Don't do it, she told herself. She couldn't seriously be considering getting involved with Devlin Sinclair, could she? Not getting involved, she corrected herself. Just having wild sex with him.

Taking a firm grip on her unruly imagination, she shook her head. Stupid idea. They worked together. The last thing she needed was an office affair, especially with her primary rival. She didn't think she'd misinterpreted the signs, either. She could tell when a man wanted her. But she had a feeling that sex wasn't the only item on Sinclair's agenda. If only it were.

For the five hundredth time, she remembered what kissing him had been like. If he'd thrown her into meltdown with a kiss, what would—?

Forget about that, she ordered herself. Try for once to think logically about the situation. What did he expect to get out of this? Beyond the obvious, of course. He'd made his suspicions about her and Franco clear. Maybe he thought that if they slept together she'd confide in him—and that would give him the upper hand. Or it could all be typical male reaction to a challenge. He'd made a move—more than one—and she hadn't immediately succumbed to his charms. The ultimate competitor, a good-looking male defense attorney. Her resistance to him had to rankle. Fortresses to be breached and all that.

But what if the seducer became the seduced? If she could cloud his thinking, then *she'd* have the upper hand. Finding the thought marvelously appealing, she smiled wickedly.

"Plotting something?" he asked her.

Halting beside her car, she slanted him a mischievous look. "Do I look like I'm plotting?"

He turned her to face him, holding her arms lightly. "You look"—he traced two fingers over her mouth—"tempting as hell." His eyes had darkened. He gazed at her but made no move to kiss her. Yet.

Devlin knew exactly what he did to women, Gabrielle mused. No man who looked like he did could be unaware of his power. He was a master of the game. The maestro of smooth moves. Had he ever let a woman get to him? She seriously doubted it, and she knew an ardent wish to give him back some of what he dished out.

Could she? The challenge was irresistible. "You know what Oscar Wilde said," she murmured, deliberately speaking in a husky whisper.

Devlin drew her closer. Despite her best efforts, her heartbeat sped up. A sizzle of tension stretched its sultry tentacles between them.

"No, what did he say?" he asked, his voice as husky as hers.

She lifted her chin and met his gaze with a

smoky challenge in her own. "The only way to get rid of a temptation is to yield to it."

He smiled, the slow, sexy smile she knew made women want to rip off their clothes for him. And dammit, it had the same effect on her. His eyes darkened to a charcoal-gray. Slowly, he lowered his head until his lips covered hers. Bent on rocking his boat, she wrapped her arms around his neck and kissed him back with an intensity intended to shoot him straight into hormonal overdrive.

For a brief, shining instant she tasted victory in his surprised reaction. And then she couldn't think at all. His arms tightened around her and his mouth grew firmer, his tongue answering the taunting movements of hers with bold thrusts of its own. His hands slid down to cup her bottom and pull her firmly against him. Dimly, she thought about stopping him, about pulling back, but her blood hummed, her heart pounded as if a freight train lived in her chest, her skin tingled. She ached as she hadn't in years . . . if ever.

He continued to kiss her, to explore her mouth with his tongue, to tantalize her with a nibble of her lips, a sharp nip, another deep, bone-melting kiss. All the while his hands roamed slowly, suggestively over her bottom. Her mind chanted a distant warning but her body melted like a snow cone in the Texas sun.

Gabrielle groaned and gripped his shoulders, then slid her hands down to his chest. His muscles felt sleek and powerful, like those of a cougar. Not at all like those of a lawyer who sat in a courtroom or read briefs all day long. She wanted to touch him, touch bare, warm skin, feel its heat against her own. Unconsciously, her fingers kneaded his chest and she angled her mouth to deepen the kiss. Drowning, she started to go under for the third time.

His mouth still fused to hers, Devlin boosted her onto the hood of her car with a move so easy, so practiced, she knew he'd done it a thousand times before. And she didn't care. His hands covered her breasts. Shaping them, molding them, caressing them. Her nipples stiffened beneath his palms. She whimpered against his mouth, not realizing she'd done it until his mouth left hers, and she moaned again when she felt his teeth nip at her neck.

Leaning her back, his body heavy on hers, he trailed his lips down her throat, pressed a hot, wet kiss into the hollow at its base, then skimmed the skin of her chest just above the cleavage. His hand slipped under her skirt and between her thighs, smoothing over the soft skin above her stockings, gliding closer to the source of her heat, closer to the sweet ache of longing. In the dim mist of her mind she heard a noise, an annoying, distant clanging.

Opening her eyes slowly, she gazed into dark gray eyes, fathoms deep with desire. Her gaze lifted, and she looked upward, confused by the harsh, glaring light, the steel beams, the hard feel of metal beneath her back. Again she heard the clanging sound and finally placed it. A car running over something.

Sanity returned, as harsh and cold as the lights. What in the devil was she doing? This wasn't her plan at all. She was supposed to be in charge here. Yet she was lying on the hood of her car in the garage parking lot, for God's sake. Moments away from being thoroughly debauched.

"Stop," she said, panting. "Devlin, wait. We can't—" He cut her off with a kiss, his lips hard against hers. Helpless for the moment, she responded, but then, grasping at what little will she had left, she wrenched her mouth away from his. "Don't. We have to stop."

Devlin stared at her, his hand still beneath her skirt, for a moment looking as dazed as she felt. But she didn't believe he could be. He was too calm, too composed. Too damned experienced to be rocked as she had been. Already the look had faded from his eyes.

"All right." Very slowly, he dragged his hand down her thigh, leaving her aware of each agonizing, taunting inch of his journey, and placed a hand on either side of her hips. His voice was seductive, as deep and dark as the devil. "Come to my place."

She shoved him away and bounded off the car before she could do anything else stupid. Like agree. "No." Striving for composure, she pushed her hair back, tucking it behind her ears. In a firmer voice she repeated the word. "No."

His eyes narrowed as he regarded her. His expression hardened. The line of his jaw tightened, as did his lips. Her heart began to thud again, from fear this time. Made uneasy by his continued silence, by the way he looked at her, she said, "Just because I let you kiss me doesn't mean—"

His harsh laughter interrupted her. "Let me? Sweetheart, you melted into a hot puddle of honey. You were as much a participant in what just happened as I was." He took a step forward. Gabrielle took two steps back.

His expression changed from angry to thunderstruck. "What's the matter with you? Do you think I'm going to attack you?"

"I-I-" She stammered and fell silent, shaking her head. Oh God, this was getting worse by the second. Why did she always do idiotic things around him?

"You do. My God, you really think I would." He stepped close to her, crowding her, overpowering her with his presence. His scent surrounded her, heady, masculine, potent. A throb of fury trembled in the air.

Her temper flared at his words. "Don't act so sanctimonious. Men do this sort of thing all the time. I ought to know, I've defended several of them. You're staring at me, looking like murder. What am I supposed to think?"

If anything, he appeared even angrier. But she felt a brief surge of . . . shame? Why should she be ashamed of a perfectly reasonable reaction?

Sarcasm laced his voice. "You can relax, sweetheart. I think I can manage to restrain myself." He took a step nearer, almost but not quite touching her, his lips curving into a hard smile when she didn't back away. "I don't have to force women. They come to my bed willingly, or not at all. Don't confuse me with your clients." With that, he turned on his heel and left her.

Infuriated, Gabrielle watched him go. She kicked at her tire, then grabbed her foot, swearing at the pain. Normally she took care to let a man know exactly where she stood, but her relationship with Devlin was anything but normal. When it came to him she had a split personality. Her mind said, "Wait, this is stupid," and her body said, "To hell with that. Go for it." It was the first time she could remember that her body and her mind were totally at odds with each other.

Though tempted to ignore the insistent ringing of her doorbell, Gabrielle didn't. Hobbling on one shoe, the other one clutched in her hand, she stalked toward the door. Rocky weaved around her legs, tripping her along the way. Bleary-eyed, she cursed halfheartedly at the dog. Her foul humor was Devlin's fault. She'd spent half the night tossing and turning and still hadn't decided what she was going to do about him. Trying to smooth things over would be the reasonable way to go, but she desperately wanted to bury the scene in oblivion.

The doorbell's repeatedly cheerful chime tempted her to throw something. She cursed again as she stumbled over the dog. Mr. Weber, she thought. Who else would it be at 7:00 A.M.? The man loved to come over and hassle her before she left for work, complaining about her trees dropping gum balls on his perfectly manicured lawn, or Rocky's barking, or anything else he could find to nag about. He needed to get a life, she thought, and geared up to tell him so.

Yanking open the door, she pointed her shoe at him and began, "Mr. Weber—"

Franco. His identity registered with a shock, and she instinctively tried to shut the door in his face. He shoved past her, smirking.

"Gabriela, really. I only came to thank you for getting me out of jail."

"How did you—?" Stupid question, she thought, halting in midsentence. Franco could find her house easily enough. "Get out. If you want to talk to me, call me at the office."

He shook his head pityingly. "Why so hostile, Gabriela?"

"You know why. Don't play innocent, Franco. That's the last thing you could ever be."

"I'm deeply wounded," he said, covering his heart with his hand. "Is that any way to treat your oldest friend?"

More like her worst nightmare. "Cut the crap. What do you want?" Taking a deep breath, she strove for control. She was overreacting, and she knew it. At least he thought she was angry. She'd be damned if she'd let him know how much he frightened her.

"A little matter you won't want made public," he answered. "A private conversation, *bellisima*."

His smile didn't reach his eyes. It never had, except a very few times . . . *Don't remember*, she told herself. She forced away the images flashing in her mind, concentrating on the present, not the past. It wasn't a great deal better.

Trapped for the moment, Gabrielle bit the inside of her cheek, welcoming the distraction of the pain. "Make it quick, I'm running late." She heard an odd rumble, a sound she couldn't place at first. Against her leg, she felt Rocky quivering and looked down at her. Hackles raised, the dog growled and bristled, staring balefully at Franco. Gabrielle almost fell over from surprise. To her knowledge, Rocky had never so much as bared her teeth at a human before. The growl grew harsher, coming from deeper in the chest. She put a hand on the big dog's collar, aware of what could happen if Rocky attacked. Her other hand clenched around the navy pump in her hand.

"Hurry up," she said. "I don't think my dog likes you."

Franco curled his lip. "Put it out."

"Drop dead." She met his gaze, knowing they were both remembering another time, another dog. Her grip tightened on Rocky's collar, the leather biting into her palm and fingers. "Why are you here?" Knowing Franco, he had a gun or a knife hidden under his dark suit. Gabrielle knew Franco's capabilities with guns. And knives. Especially knives. But she wouldn't back down.

He smiled again, though less easily, and took a seat. His expression sincere, he looked up at her. "I must talk to you about Vito."

"I told you, I won't discuss Vito with you."

"He's very ill. If I could tell him that I've seen you, that you've asked about him . . ."

"Ill?" In spite of herself, it worried her. But Franco could be lying, very likely was. "What's wrong with him?"

Franco lifted a shoulder. "The doctors don't seem to know. For myself, I think it's a broken heart."

She snorted. "Get real. Vito's one of the least sentimental people I've ever known. If he's pining, it isn't for me, it's because he lost a pawn. And I doubt he's still concerned over something that happened years ago."

"Do you really think he's forgotten you? You know you're more to him than a pawn."

Was she? It didn't matter. That part of her life was finished. She frowned, narrowing her eyes at him. Or it would be finished, once she got rid of

Franco. "If that's all you've got to say, you can leave now."

"Wait! Gabriela, if you'd see him it would mean the world to him."

And what would it mean to Franco if he came back with her in tow? Did he think her so stupid, she couldn't see what he was up to? Play it cool, she thought. Don't let him see how he gets to you. "It's too late for Vito and me. Besides, I'm stuck here working on your case, remember?"

"After that. Come back with me."

She stared at him, awed by his nerve. "Are you nuts? I wouldn't go to a dog fight with you." Though he covered it quickly, she saw the anger flash in his eyes. His looks and, even more, his power didn't garner him many rejections. But she knew the real Franco. The soulless monster who lived behind the smooth, darkly handsome exterior.

Noxious sincerity oozing from every pore, he asked, "Was it so bad between us?" His voice dropped to a deeper tone. "Don't you remember any of the good?"

"Franco, there was never an 'us.' There was me and there was you and Vito. I was merely a pawn in your struggle for power."

"I loved you, Gabriela."

She closed her eyes, willing the nausea down. Opening them, she said harshly, "You've never cared spit for anyone but yourself. Least of all a woman. Now get out." She gestured at the door with her shoe, holding it like a would-be sword. "And don't do this again. I can still quit your case."

His smile was knowing.

Her eyebrow lifted, and she gazed at him coolly. "Do you think I won't?"

"You don't dare risk it." Softly, he asked, "What will CG and S do when they find out you're the daughter of Vito Donati? The missing Mafia heiress. The woman everyone believes is dead."

Malice curled around her with each of his words. Gabrielle couldn't stop the sudden intake of her breath, though the threat was no surprise. She'd be out on her butt faster than a revolving door. But she wouldn't buckle under to Franco's threats. Not without a fight. "Fine. You tell them. But get ready for jail, because I swear if you expose me, I'll make sure that you rot there for the rest of your life. I promise you, I can do it."

He shook his head, his expression sympathetic. "You misunderstand. We'll talk more later, when you're not so distraught. But I would never do anything to hurt you, Gabriela." He rose and strode to the door.

Once there, he turned back to look at her. Handsome, powerful, he donned the guise of a charming businessman as easily as changing clothes. But Gabrielle saw the blood dripping from his hands.

He smiled and met her gaze. "Unless, of course, you force me to."

The door closed behind him. Gabrielle relaxed

her death grip on Rocky's collar, and the dog lunged at the door, barking and growling furiously. "I know just how you feel," Gabrielle said, sinking into a chair and burying her head in her hands. "God, what am I going to do now?"

SIX

Devlin checked his watch for the fifth time that morning. 9:30 A.M. He didn't need a crystal ball to tell him that it was unusual for Gabrielle to be late. They were supposed to interview Sabatino's alibis and character witnesses that day. Character witness. That was a joke when it came to Sabatino. In any event, Devlin had wanted to get an early start. But he wondered if he was ticked because he and Gabrielle had a lot of ground to cover that day, or because he was still chapped by what hadn't happened the night before?

Devlin acknowledged he hadn't behaved particularly well, but then, neither had Gabrielle. His behavior bothered him more than hers, though. Being hot for her was fine. Perfectly understandable, a normal male reaction to a sexy, beautiful woman. What irritated the hell out of him was that she made him crazy. Almost . . . out of control.

After a lifetime of watching his mother manipulate his father, he'd promised himself that no woman would ever pull his strings.

But he wasn't his father and, God help him, he never would be. Besides, Devlin knew the answer to his problem. Once he got Gabrielle into his bed, he could get her out of his head.

Glancing up at the knock on his door, he frowned and snapped out a clipped, "It's open."

"Sorry I'm late," Gabrielle said upon entering. "Are you ready to leave?"

The sight of her was a balm to his wounded pride. Dark circles under her eyes, her hair escaping the usual neat twist, one earring. Not her office standard, the put-together, buttoned-up-tighter-than-a-nun image. Feeling magnanimous, he decided to make her apology easier for her. "Yeah, in a minute." He rose, keeping his gaze on her. She looked like she hadn't had an hour of sleep the night before. "I'm sorry about last night."

"Last night?" She echoed his words blankly, her forehead furrowing. He could swear it wasn't an act. After a moment her brow cleared. "Oh, that. Let's just forget it happened."

Forget it? His jaw damn near dropped to his chest. Forget it? Like hell he would. She'd melted into a gooey puddle the night before and now she couldn't even remember it? Devlin wanted to strangle her.

No, he wanted her begging for mercy. Begging for him.

He shrugged, pretending indifference. "Sure. Consider it forgotten. Let's hit the road."

Before he reached the door, it opened and a woman tumbled in. Lank blond hair hung to her shoulders. Bruised, battered, wearing a ragged T-shirt and threadbare blue jeans, she stood like a homeless waif in the middle of his doorway. Marcie, he realized with a sinking feeling. From the looks of her, she hadn't managed to get rid of the lowlife bastard who lived with her, either.

Her words rushed out before he could stop them. "Mr. Sinclair, I'm so glad you're here. I know I should've waited, but the receptionist didn't believe me when I told her you were my lawyer. I've seen the look before, and I knew she'd keep me sitting there forever before she even told you I was here." Her eyes beseeched him to understand. "So I sneaked in when she left her desk."

"It's okay, Marcie," he said, bringing her inside and closing the door behind her. "What's wrong?"

She twisted her hands together and paced. "I tried, I did, but he wouldn't listen. See what happened when I told him?" On the verge of tears, she pointed to her black eye and bruised cheek. "What am I gonna do?" she wailed.

Crap. Frowning, he stuck his hands in his pockets. Just what he didn't need right now. Turning to Gabrielle, he said, "I'll take care of this and then we'll go. It won't take long." He waited for her to leave, but she didn't. She stared at him and Marcie with a speculative gleam in her eye.

"Take your time." She waved a hand in the air. "I'm in no rush. I'm Gabrielle Rousseau," she told Marcie, offering her hand. "One of Mr. Sinclair's colleagues."

"You're a lawyer too?"

Gabrielle smiled. "That's right. But don't let me interrupt. Go on."

Devlin interrupted. "Ms. Field might not want—"

"Oh, I don't care," Marcie said. "Just tell me what to do so I can get rid of Mark. You said if I didn't, I don't stand a chance of getting the kids back. I want my babies, I miss them." Tears coursed down her cheeks. "And Mark's getting meaner by the day."

Devlin winced. If anyone deserved to have a good cry, Marcie Field did. Even though he was accustomed to women's tears by now, they still made him uncomfortable. "We can get a restraining order issued on him." Not that it would do much good with scum like Mark White, he thought.

Gabrielle helped Marcie to a chair. Devlin leaned back against his desk and dredged up what he remembered from the last time he'd talked to her. "He still fencing for the pawnshop?"

"Says he isn't," Marcie answered morosely.

"But you think he is."

"Yeah. He's too flush not to be."

And too high, Devlin bet. "Okay. The first thing you need to do is go to that shelter I told you about." He held up a hand at her protest. "Until we get White in jail, you can't stay at that apartment. Do you want him to kill you next time?"

"If I don't get my babies back, I don't care what he does."

"Come on, Marcie, you know that's not true. Just try it. I'll tip the cops about him and the pawnshop. They'll pick him up. He won't make bail, I'll guarantee that."

"And then?"

Hope gleamed in her eyes. Good, Devlin thought. That meant she hadn't been totally beaten down. "Once we're sure White's out of your life, we'll find you a job. It's going to take a while, but we'll get your kids back."

A few minutes later, after extracting a promise to go immediately to the shelter, he saw her to the door. Devlin slipped her a couple of bills, his attempt to do it on the sly foiled when she threw her arms around him and blubbered.

Women. He should have known.

Devlin Sinclair, white knight? Gabrielle asked herself. In his car, the Beamer that screamed yuppie lawyer, on their way to their first appointment, she glanced over at him. Eyeing his profile, she noted the stubborn line of his jaw. He didn't want to discuss his client, but she didn't want to talk about Franco. She needed at least a few more minutes to pull herself together.

"I'm a little confused about your role in Marcie Field's life. If she's the one being abused, why does she need a defense counsel?"

He answered readily enough. "Different case. Her ex made her out as an unfit mother and took full custody of the kids. No visitation. I was her lawyer. She moved to Dallas after the trial."

"You lost her case?" Her eyes widened. *There* was a surprise. She didn't think Devlin ever lost.

He shot her an irritated glance. "It happens. The bastard paid off half the city. Marcie Field didn't have a prayer."

"You're still trying to help her."

"Can we get back to the case at hand? Sabatino, remember him?"

She accepted the change of subject because he gave her no choice. Yet the idea of Devlin Sinclair actually having a heart still shocked her. What else went on behind the scenes that he preferred to keep silent? "Who's the first interview?"

"Caleb Bailey. You know, the guy who was originally the prosecution's witness. Sabatino allegedly extorted protection money from him."

"Until he changed his mind and refused to testify against Sabatino," Gabrielle said. "Now I wonder what made him do that?" she added sarcastically.

Devlin shrugged. "Doesn't matter. We need to see if he'll be a credible witness for the defense."

Late that afternoon, on the way back to the office, Gabrielle pondered the events of the day. Caleb Bailey, and every other witness they had interviewed that day, was useless. Not a decent one in the bunch. Bailey had been so frightened, he shook, and Gabrielle doubted he'd be any better in a courtroom. Worse, if anything. While it didn't break her heart not to find any reputable witnesses for the defense, she knew Devlin would come up with something. Why did he have to be so good? Her lip curled in a snarl of irritation.

Franco deserved to be in jail, she thought. Should have been a long time ago. It would do the world a favor if—

"Hey, are you in there?" Devlin asked, one hand on the wheel, the other touching her arm.

She jerked in surprise. "Sorry. I was thinking."

He cast her a considered look. "I said we'll try the police reports next. Maybe they screwed up on something."

Get him off on a technicality? It wasn't a new tactic; she'd used it herself. The problem was, she didn't want Franco to get off. "I'll start going over them tonight," she offered.

"No hurry. Tomorrow will be soon enough. We'll keep the teams looking for more witnesses, though. Some miracle might turn up."

With Franco's luck it would, Gabrielle thought. Back in the office a short while later, she couldn't concentrate on anything. Trying to work was a lost cause, but she couldn't generate a lot of enthusiasm for going home, either.

She'd just about decided to leave when Nina

stuck her head in the office doorway. "Hey, Gabrielle, check out Alfonso's with me. Half an hour, okay?"

"Thanks, Nina, but I—"

"You can't turn me down. One drink—I've got a date later. Wait until I tell you about this guy."

Nina and her men, Gabrielle thought as her friend disappeared before she could answer. Alfonso's. After the day she'd had, she could use some relaxation.

Gabrielle had intended to leave the bar as soon as Nina's date showed up, but she couldn't force herself to go home and face the silence. Or the memories she knew would swamp her once she let down her guard. Even her music, she knew, wouldn't provide solace that night. Seeking distraction, she glanced around at the clientele of the well-filled bar, an oddly soothing proliferation of professionals. One of her colleagues' favorite hangouts, it attracted bankers, doctors, CEO's, and other assorted upscale types. And no doubt a Mafia hit man or two, disguised as something else, she reminded herself sourly. Still, being there kept her mind going instead of stalling on finding a solution to disaster.

Her life, the disaster. Franco's conviction would solve everything. Or if not everything, a large portion of it. They would put him away for years. But how to accomplish that? Short of turning over evidence to the prosecution . . . Despite her initial disgust at the thought, the idea took root. Logs, records, address books. She and Devlin had a number of them that the prosecution would never see. An anonymous tip—

No! She couldn't do it. Unethical, certainly. Illegal too. She was bound by law and her professional oath to protect her client. And if she quit the case, there went her only power over Franco. The power to see him freed . . . or convicted.

Could she do it? Gabrielle asked herself. With a gulp, she drained her wine, then signaled to the bartender for a second one. Could she really commit an act that would get her disbarred? *Only if someone finds out*, a little voice reminded her. That was pure fright speaking, she knew, but just now she was all tapped out of courage.

If no one knew and she made certain that Franco stayed behind bars, all her problems would vanish. She shook her head sharply, biting her lip. No, she couldn't do it. Risk disbarment, risk her career? But if she didn't—

"Buy you a drink?" a male voice asked.

Gabrielle turned her head. A man she'd never met before stood beside her, smiling. He didn't really look like Franco, other than having the misfortune of being dark-haired and dark-skinned. Lacking the energy to be polite, she chose the quickest route to getting rid of him.

"Get lost."

He didn't take the hint. He pulled up a stool

and parked his fanny on it like he meant to stay forever. "What's a pretty lady like you doing here all by your lonesome?"

Now that's original, she thought. "Drinking. Alone," she said, and turned her head. The man kept talking but she blocked the sound out, her thoughts returning to the cause of her misery. If Franco was convicted due to her machinations, that made her no better than him. She shuddered and downed half her wine. No better than Franco.

Did she have another choice? Of course she did. There was always a choice.

Gabrielle decided to choose to forget about it. She was halted at a dead end, anyway. Though just for a night, she told herself, and raised the glass to her lips.

After her third glass of wine, the tingling sensation the alcohol gave her reminded her of the feeling she got every time a certain attorney touched her. She'd succeeded in pushing Franco to the back of her mind, but Devlin Sinclair was a whole 'nother story. What would happen if she quit worrying about his angles and schemes and just . . . did what she wanted to do? Sober, she would have called it a stupid idea, but right now it held tremendous appeal.

A hand fell on her shoulder. Hadn't she run that guy off yet? She swung around and snapped, "You want to lose that hand?"

"Not particularly," a deep, familiar voice said. "Touchy, aren't you?"

"You." Gabrielle blinked and attempted to focus. It was Devlin, with an eat-your-heart-out smile lilting on his mouth. He looked hazy. And delicious. Every single one of her nerve endings jumped in anticipation. Temptation.

"In the flesh," he said, and pulled up the empty stool beside her.

SEVEN

"Is that your standard bar procedure?" Devlin asked Gabrielle, letting the hand in question linger on her shoulder. She'd let her hair down, he noticed. It flowed in dark, rich waves to her shoulders, looking as if she'd shoved her hands through it. Or someone else had. Would it look like that after she'd just gotten out of bed?

She smiled, a slow, sexy smile he hadn't seen on her face before. Devlin sucked in a breath, feeling like all four volumes of the Texas Legal Directory had landed on his stomach.

"I only threaten men with bad lines who try to pick me up." Her tone matched her smile.

To give himself a moment to think, Devlin signaled the bartender. Thankfully, his brain did begin functioning again. He'd been afraid all the blood had rushed to other parts of his anatomy. "That lets me out, then. I've got a dynamite line."

She laughed and shook her head. "Do you? I wouldn't have thought you'd need one."

Whatever had gotten into her, he liked her in this mood. He blessed the impulse that had led him to Alfonso's after overhearing Nina's invitation to Gabrielle. "I can't decide if that's a compliment or an insult."

Her lips curved upward, but she didn't speak. Devlin ordered for both of them and turned back to her.

"Okay," she said, "let's hear it."

"What, the line?"

"No, the Gettysburg Address. Of course the line." She flicked him another killer smile. "Bet I've heard it before."

Devlin grinned. God, he loved a challenge. "How much?"

"This round's on the loser."

"Deal." He put out his hand, and they shook.

"Have at it, Romeo." Pulling her hand away, she turned her back to him.

Devlin touched her shoulder. In a replay of a few minutes earlier, she swung around, pure frost in her eyes. "Excuse me, ma'am," he said, "you wouldn't happen to have a condom on you, would you?"

"Sorry. I don't have the anatomy for it."

Devlin gave a shout of laughter. "Damn, you've heard it before."

Grinning, she arched an eyebrow. "Actually, no. But I'm quick." Just then the bartender set their drinks in front of them. "Put them on my tab," she told him.

Devlin toasted her with his Scotch and water. "To fast comebacks."

"And bad lines." She rested her chin in her hand and looked at him earnestly. "I think you need serious help with your definition of dynamite."

"I won the bet, didn't I?"

"Winning isn't everything," she stated in a pious tone.

"Beats the hell out of losing." He slid his arm across the back of her bar stool. "If I wanted to get a beautiful woman's attention"—he caught her gaze and smiled, the smile guaranteed to make a woman weak-kneed and willing—"that's not what I'd ask her."

"What would you say, then?"

Did she know her voice had softened? His hand trailed up to the back of her neck, sneaking under her hair. He lowered his voice to midnight quiet and held her gaze. "Aren't you the woman I dreamed about last night?"

Her eyes widened; he heard her breath catch. "That might work," she admitted huskily, after a moment.

"Did it?" His hand continued its caress, tracing slow, sensual circles on her neck.

"It's a . . . definite possibility."

"I've never used it before."

"Never?" Her voice was almost a whisper. He had to strain to hear it.

"No." He leaned in close, so close, their mouths were nearly touching. So close, he felt her breath feather across his lips. The chatter, the music, the people surrounding them faded to black. "The thing is"—he picked up her hand and brushed the lightest of kisses over the backs of her fingers—"it's not a line. It happens to be true."

Their gazes still locked, Gabrielle drew in a deep, unsteady breath. Her eyes turned a bottomless, misty green. For a long moment neither spoke. "You're very good," she breathed. "I almost believe you."

"Believe it," he said, and moved in for the kill.

His mouth was a sigh away from hers when she jerked her head back and yanked her hand from his. The moment shattered like thin ice.

"You win," she said, and reached for her wine.

Watching her gulp some down, Devlin smiled. The spell had broken, but the aftereffects remained. "What's this? Gabrielle Rousseau, CG and S's finest, conceding so easily?"

"I'm having an off night."

"Drowning your sorrows?"

"No, no, no." She toasted him with her glass. "Celebrating. It's much more fun."

He had to give it to her, she made a quick recovery. "What are you celebrating? The Sabatino case isn't exactly going ninety to nothing. For our side, anyway."

"Oh, that." Waving one hand dismissively, she finished off half the wine. "We'll find something. So what if he's got lousy character witnesses?"

"It makes defen—"

Before he could finish the sentence she interrupted. "You surprised me today, you know?" Leaning forward with the glass in her hand tilting precariously to one side, she dropped her voice to a conspiratorial whisper. "Ms. . . . whatever, can't remember her name. The woman who came to see you this morning. Why'd you take her case?"

Hello? Where did that come from? Devlin wondered. Drinking some of his Scotch, he considered her. Apparently Gabrielle didn't want to talk about Sabatino. And he didn't care to talk about Marcie Field. Not answering would only make her more curious, so to appease her he gave her something. "She needed a lawyer. What's to understand?"

"That lady is pro bono all the way, Shinclair."

His lips quirked at the slurred word. She stared at him intently, obviously unaware of her lapse. "Everybody does a little pro bono work," he said. "You do, don't you?"

"Certainly." She gave an emphatic nod and took another sip of wine. "But you"—she poked him in the chest with her forefinger—"aren't the type. Not a pro bono bone in your body. You don't have to counsel for free, not at this stage of your career. So why?"

Not the type, he repeated silently. Devlin gave

in to the irresistible urge to shock her out of her smug reading of his character. "I was a PD for three years." Her finger fell, and her mouth dropped open. Though he smiled, her disbelief annoyed him more than it amused him. "Just out of law school," he added.

"You? A public defender?" She stared in amazement, then threw her head back and laughed.

Her throaty, abandoned laughter brought on a curious range of feelings. Lust at the sight of her slim neck, exposed as it was, and at the rich sound of her enjoyment. Intense, and irritating, disappointment that she'd reacted as she had. Why should he be surprised that she only saw what everyone else saw? And why the hell should he care? Sipping his drink, he waited for her paroxysm to subside.

Abruptly, she sobered and put her hand on his arm. "I'm sorry." A hiccup lessened the effect of her apology. She continued doggedly. "You were so good with your client today. It shouldn't have shocked me, I guess. But I can't—couldn't imag—"

"Yeah, I know." He gave her a cynical smile. "It doesn't fit the image."

Tilting her head, she gazed at him, as though trying to piece together a puzzle. "If the image bothers you, why don't you change it?"

He shrugged. "It doesn't bother me. I'm not a PD anymore."

"Maybe part of you still is," she said shrewdly. Devlin didn't like the direction this conversation had taken. He'd outgrown that particular save-the-world mind-set long ago. Three years as a PD would polish off anyone's idealism, and finding out the truth about Celine had sounded the death knell on his. Remembering Celine sure as hell held no interest for him. "Nope," he answered. "What you see is what you get."

She hadn't taken her hand off his arm. He'd left his jacket in the car, and her fingers pressed gently into his skin, warming it through the cloth of his shirtsleeve. There was no reason for that innocent contact to send a surge of desire pumping through his blood. No reason at all.

"I wonder," she said.

"And I wonder," he said, taking the offensive, "what it is about Sabatino that gets to you. You've defended others like him. But there's a difference this time, isn't there, Gabrielle?"

Her hand dropped away. A gleam of alarm came and went in her eyes, so quickly, he might have imagined it. Except he hadn't.

"I've got a lot more at stake this time," she said.

"Somehow, that doesn't surprise me. Care to let me in on the stakes?"

Her lashes lowered, then rose, her expression changing to sultry. Even knowing her game, it still sent his hormone level rocketing.

"Winner take all. Partner."

Devlin let out a breath he hadn't been aware of holding. Damn, she was good.

"But tonight"—she stroked her hand up his arm—"I don't want to talk about Sabatino." Her hand glided slowly down to his. "Or partnerships. Or law. I'm taking the night off. What do you say, Counselor?"

An invitation. In her eyes, in her touch, in her words. So, she wanted to distract him, did she? Just how far would she go?

"That depends." He took her hand, running his thumb along the inside of her wrist. Her pulse scrambled, and he smiled. "What did you have in mind?"

She touched her tongue to her lips in a nervous, unconsciously sensual gesture. "Oh God, I think I'm in trouble."

Her voice sounded like the night, a husky whisper of pure temptation. Devlin smiled and said nothing. He unbuttoned her sleeve and trailed his fingers up her arm as he pushed the material higher. Her lips parted on a moan that she caught just before completion. Strangely, his own pulse was none too steady. Just from touching her arm? Listening to her voice? Get a grip, he told himself.

She stared at him and licked her lips again. "Now I know I'm in trouble. I can't . . . I can't . . ."

When he touched his lips to the pulse throbbing at the crook of her arm, her breath hissed in with a gasp. "Can't what?" he murmured, lingering over the magnolia petal skin of her arm.

"I can't think when you do that." Dazed dark-green eyes stared at him.

"Don't think, then." He threw some money on the bar to cover the check and rose, pulling her to her feet. "Come on. Let's get out of here." Grasping her hand, he didn't wait for her answer, but dragged her along with him.

Outside, the night air was hot, humid. Clear and sultry as only a Southern summer night can be. Late as it was, the street in front of the bar was devoid of traffic. They crossed it quickly, almost silently, their shoes scraping on the rough pavement. An ambulance siren wailed in the distance. Reaching his car, Devlin pushed her back against the door and stared at her good and long. She hadn't spoken a word since he'd hauled her out of the bar. He couldn't say what prompted him to ask the next question, because he didn't want to hear it if her answer was no.

"Are you sure about this?"

She didn't answer with words. Instead she wrapped her arms around his neck and kissed him, a woman who knew what she wanted and meant to get it. He drew her closer, until he felt her breasts crushed to his chest, the welcome pressure as he cupped her bottom and settled her tightly against him. Sweet and wicked at once, she tasted of temptation and midnight sin.

And she kissed like a fantasy lover. Her tongue darted inside his mouth, teasing, arousing, flirting with him and begging for more. He caressed her bottom, drawing her even closer, and met her tongue's parries with some lingering thrusts of his own. The blood pounded in his veins, and he shot straight into sensual overload. If he didn't stop kissing her now, they'd be courting a public indecency charge in a matter of minutes.

"The next time I kiss you," he said, indulging in a last caress at the corner of her mouth, "you'll be wearing a lot fewer clothes."

"Is that a threat or a promise?"

Smiling, he unlocked the car door and let her in. "A promise."

He didn't ask, but drove to her place since it was a good five minutes closer. Right now five minutes seemed like a long time. Devlin couldn't remember wanting to make love with a woman this badly. Ever. Even half-crazed from lust, it worried him. But not enough to make him forget the idea.

Not eager to wreck his car on the way, he kept his hands off her. Gabrielle had no such worries. She scooted over as close as the bucket seats would allow and snuggled her head against his shoulder. It surprised him, because it bespoke affection rather than passion, but her hand on his thigh wasn't innocent by a long shot.

"Are you trying to make me have a wreck?" he asked, barely maintaining control.

"Drive faster." She kissed his neck and trailed wicked fingers over his thigh.

"My insurance—" he began, and sucked in his breath as her hand caressed him, edging so close to his erection, he thought he'd die. To hell with insurance rates, he thought, and put his foot down.

They made it inside her house before he started ripping her clothes off. Barely. He pushed her up against the door and kissed her, possessing her mouth as he wanted to possess her entire body. Fumbling at the buttons of her blouse, he felt as if it were the first time he'd ever undressed a woman. Slow down, he told himself, but he wasn't sure he could. Where were all his practiced moves?

The flesh-colored wisp of a Midnight and Lace specialty demi-bra cupped her breasts like a lover's hands. Devlin popped the clasp open and spread the bra wide, watching her nipples tighten under his scrutiny. Beautiful breasts, lush, full, with dusky rose areolas begging for him to taste them. He bent his head and took a taut peak in his mouth, sucking, swirling his tongue over the tip while she moaned his name. Her hands were in his hair, clutching his head tightly to her breasts.

"Devlin." This time she gasped it. "We—I—"

She groaned as he trailed his lips to her other breast, slid his hand under her skirt, and dipped it inside her panties. His fingers slipped over her slick, warm skin, before he parted her feminine flesh and thrust a finger inside. She was paradise. Hot, wet, and waiting for him.

"I need to . . . lie down." Another moan came, steamy and low in her throat as he caressed her. "Devlin." Her hands gripped and released his shoulders convulsively, until he became aware of where they were and what he was doing.

He was about to take her standing up against the door. God, he was a jerk, but not that big of a jerk. He kissed her mouth and swung her up in his arms, praying the bedroom wasn't far. A few moments later he laid her on the bed and followed her down, his aching flesh resting firmly against her burgeoning warmth. Her hands slid over his shoulders again, then fell back to the bed. Devlin buried his face in her neck, breathed in her scent, somewhere between sweet and spicy and uniquely hers. She felt soft, so soft. Boneless and willing beneath him.

Craving the taste of her, he sucked her nipple, rolled it with his tongue. She groaned and arched her back, her breast rising up to meet him. Her skin like satin against his lips, he tasted the underside of one breast as he moved to the other. She was completely relaxed, languorous, his to do with as he'd been dreaming about since he met her.

His conscience set up an annoying buzz that he tried unsuccessfully to ignore. Devlin raised his head from her breasts and looked at Gabrielle. In the indirect lighting thrown from the hallway, he could see that her eyes were closed. Willing? he asked himself. Or drunk?

"Open your eyes," he demanded, staring down at her. Her lips were swollen, rosy and inviting.

Slowly her lids fluttered open. Deep green eyes, hazy, unfocused.

She hadn't seemed that drunk in the bar. Loosened up, maybe, but not drunk. Right, his interfering alter ego argued. That's why last night she said no and tonight she's jumping your bones, you idiot. Perfectly reasonable.

"What made you change your mind?"

Still hazy, she gazed at him, smiling. Then she giggled.

Giggling was a bad sign. A very bad sign. He put his hands on her shoulders and gave her a gentle shake. "Gabrielle, answer me. Why tonight? Why not last night?"

"D'licious." She ran her tongue over her lips and giggled again. "Ir-re-sistible."

Worse and worse. He groaned and rested his forehead against hers. Delicious? Irresistible? The Gabrielle he knew would never have said that. Unless she'd imbibed too much of that wine. The giggling clinched it.

Why the sudden attack of scruples? he asked himself. She was a grown woman. Even drunk, she was bound to have realized what would happen.

"Kiss me," she demanded.

Her mouth, not to mention her body, tempted the hell out of him.

"Kiss me," she whispered again, putting her arms around his neck.

So he kissed her, doing his best to block out everything but the feel of her beneath him, the sweet lingering taste of her flesh, of her mouth. It didn't work. He stopped kissing her and looked at her again. Crap. She was so vulnerable, so trusting, he knew he couldn't do it. Why did he think of Gabrielle as vulnerable? She was the Queen of Sharks. The least vulnerable woman he knew.

Was this his punishment for all of the lousy things he'd ever done in his life? The conscience he thought he didn't have had picked a hell of a time to go active on him.

Cursing under his breath, he rolled off her and sat up. Her eyes had closed again. A faint smile curved those luscious lips. Her clothes were a disaster, half on, half off, twisted around her slim body. If he didn't do something, she'd sleep all night like that. Devlin couldn't fathom why that bothered him, or comprehend the urge to take care of her.

He hit pay dirt the second drawer he opened, but shut it after only a moment's perusal. Noble intentions be damned if he put her in one of those sexy nightgowns. Instead, he scrounged up a T-shirt. The sight of her nearly nude had him questioning his sanity, but he finally got her stripped, into the shirt, and tucked into her bed. Alone.

You shouldn't be so trusting, he told her silently, bending to brush a kiss across her lips. Not of him. Devlin still couldn't believe he was walking away from her.

"Nice," she mumbled, and burrowed deeper

into the covers. She opened her eyes and stared straight at him. "You're a nice man." Her eyes drifted shut and her breathing deepened, became regular. Dreamland.

Devlin had been called a lot of things by a lot of women, but he couldn't remember nice ever being one of them.

EIGHT

A jackhammer pounded a full-volume symphony of misery in her head. And her stomach. Better not to even think about that. Gabrielle groaned, rolled out of bed, and faceplanted on the floor. Flashes of memory from the night before came back to her as she lay there trying to summon the will to rise.

Lord, no. Tell me I didn't. Her eyes popped open and she jerked upright, then immediately regretted the sudden movement. Looking down, she realized she wasn't naked. That would have been a good sign, except . . . she never slept in T-shirts. Which could only mean that someone else had put this T-shirt on her. Someone else being—

Oh God, it was no dream. She'd gone to bed with Devlin Sinclair the night before. Apparently had a good time of it, too, she thought, glancing around the room. Clothes were strewn everywhere, not in their usual neat stacks or hung up in the closet. Holding her throbbing head, she forced herself to go back over the evening. Alfonso's. Wine. Several glasses of wine. She groaned again. How much had she had? And Devlin, looking even more mouthwatering than usual. Oh yeah, she'd done it.

Hoping it would help clear her mind, she stumbled into the shower. Twenty minutes later, after aspirin and a shower, teeth brushed and coffee in hand, she felt almost human. But she still couldn't remember everything. Up until the moment Devlin had carried her into the bedroom, she was fairly clear, but once there . . . Get real, Gabrielle, she told herself. She'd thrown herself at him, practically ripped her clothes off and said, "Here, take me." What the hell did she *think* had happened?

How could she have been so stupid? So reckless? So irresponsible? Going to bed with Devlin didn't worry her nearly so much as not being able to remember what had happened. What she'd said, and done. What he'd said. And done.

Her stomach fluttered wildly at that last thought. Not one for self-deception, Gabrielle didn't pretend she'd slept with Devlin because she was upset or drunk. She'd done it because she wanted to, and had since she'd met him. Now if she could only *remember* it.

She never did things like this. Never had before, anyway. And blaming everything on the disastrous scene with Franco the previous morning wouldn't work, either. Being upset was no excuse for her rash behavior.

The doorbell rang. Cautiously, she peered out the peephole. Great. Two men she'd give a million bucks not to see and naturally one of them stood on her doorstep. Maybe if she pretended she wasn't home, he'd go away. No, that was the coward's way out, and she'd been enough of a coward lately to last her a lifetime.

Gabrielle swung the door open, but before she could utter a sound, Devlin hauled her into his arms and planted a long, lingering, hotter-than-sin kiss on her lips. Thirty seconds into it, her legs felt like the center of a jelly donut.

"Hi, beautiful." He drew back enough for her to catch a glimpse of laughing gray eyes before he kissed her again.

Beautiful? He made it sound sincere, even though she knew he must say it to all the women he . . . kissed. Gabrielle hung in his arms with all the backbone of a rag doll. His smile really should be outlawed, she thought, and so should the way he kissed. She found herself responding, opening her mouth, accepting his tongue, meeting it with hers. Good grief, what was she doing? Talk, don't kiss, she ordered herself. Flustered, she wedged a hand between them and shoved against his chest. "Wait," she managed to say.

Devlin loosened his hold, but kept his arms around her. Gabrielle caught her breath and wished his embrace didn't feel so supportive. So good.

"Yeah, you're right." He walked her backward toward the couch. "We don't have enough time for what I'd really like to do with you."

He started to kiss her again, but she pulled away, unable to halt the flush that heated her cheeks or the erotic sensations he'd provoked with his kiss. "No, I mean, we need to talk."

He glanced at his watch. "Can we do it on the way? I told the sergeant we'd be there by ten."

Mystified, she blinked at him. "Be where by ten?"

"The police station. You didn't forget we were going over the Sabatino case files, did you? The police reports."

"This morning? On a Saturday? But I can't—" Police reports, she thought. Her head throbbed, the pain returning full force. She couldn't let him go alone; she had to see those reports. "I'm not ready," she said, gesturing at her cutoffs and cropped shirt.

His gaze slid slowly down her body and back up. He might as well have used his hands instead, from the effect that long, provocative examination had on her. Her skin burned, tingled. Her stomach tightened in anticipation.

"You forgot, didn't you?" A wickedly charming smile spread across his face. "After last night I'm not surprised."

She hadn't forgotten *everything* that had happened the night before. "Hold it right there," she said, struggling to establish control. "We've got to talk before we go anywhere."

He raised an eyebrow, then shrugged. "All right. Got any more coffee?"

"Help yourself." Crossing her arms over her chest, she watched him walk out of the room. Dammit, he looked as good in blue jeans as he did in a suit. Maybe better, she admitted, admiring the way the denim hugged his rear and his long, lean legs. How could she possibly have forgotten making love with him?

"What's on your mind?" he asked when he came back and sat beside her on the couch.

Gabrielle stared at him, incapable of speech. What could she say? she realized. *By the way, Devlin, what exactly did happen last night? I seem to have passed out before the big moment.* Oh, right. Only if she was into self-flagellation and humiliation.

Bailing out, she said, "I can go over the police reports by myself, if you want. Free you up to pursue another avenue." He wouldn't go for it, she knew, but what the hell.

"It's not a problem. Besides, you don't have your car, remember? I'll drop you by Alfonso's afterward, and you can pick it up then."

Plastering a fake smile on her face, she conceded to the inevitable. "Let me change and we'll go."

"Is there something else you wanted to talk to me about?"

An innocent question. Gabrielle stopped at the hall doorway and looked at him. Why did she get the feeling he'd asked that question with a purpose in mind? His bland expression gave nothing away. "No, nothing," she said. "I won't be long."

A short while later at the police station, Gabrielle tried to keep her mind on the business at hand, but with Devlin sitting across from her it was impossible. He didn't talk, he simply read the reports, thoroughly, like any competent lawyer. But his mere presence, especially given what had happened the night before, distracted her until she could have screamed with frustration.

That might have been why she almost missed it. It should have shouted to her, even buried as it was in the back of several other records and files concerning the arrest. It was a hole big enough to drop the state of Texas into, a glaring error in the chain of custody of the evidence that practically guaranteed Franco Sabatino's case would be thrown out of court. The officer in charge of the evidence room hadn't noted the time when the evidence was transferred to him. The transportation officer's signature was there, but nowhere did it state that the evidence officer had logged the evidence in at a given time.

No familiar thrill of triumph accompanied the discovery. No sense of accomplishment, no swell of excitement that here lay the key to winning another case, the key to her career. Instead she felt sickened that she would be instrumental in making certain that, once more, Franco Sabatino escaped paying for his crimes. With this development she knew they would get him off. And she realized with stomach-churning dread and despair that there was nothing on this earth she wanted less than to see Franco Sabatino go free.

"Nothing here to get Sabatino off," Devlin muttered, flipping another page. Though he never counted on police error, it sure made his cases easier when it occurred. "Not even a hint of a glitch." He snapped the last file shut and tossed it on the table in disgust. "How about you?" he asked Gabrielle. "Find anything?"

She looked at him for a moment, blinked, then looked away. "Nothing," she said, gathering her stack of reports together and closing the files.

"Damn!" Frustrated, he slapped his hand on the table. "This isn't looking good."

"Something—" She hesitated and cleared her throat. "Something's bound to turn up."

Was it his imagination or did she look paler than she had a few minutes ago? "What enthusiasm. You sound like you'd just as soon it didn't."

"Don't be absurd," she snapped, fiddling with the files. "You're not the only one who wants to win."

Considering her, he said slowly, "I hadn't thought so." Definitely paler, he thought. Something was up with her. From what he'd seen that morning, Gabrielle hadn't been able to concentrate worth jack on anything. Tense and distracted didn't begin to describe her. He felt an unwanted flash of guilt, knowing that last night was bound to be at least part of her problem.

"What's that supposed to mean?" she asked. The words snapped out, and her head had come up belligerently. She met his gaze dead-on.

Touchy, he thought, and shrugged off her sharp question. "Nothing. Come on, let's go. We've done all we can for now."

He gathered the reports together and tucked them under his arm to give back to the sergeant. "Ready?" he asked, holding the door open and looking at her.

Their glances met again, his faintly questioning, hers revealing nothing.

"Yes," she said, and walked out ahead of him.

Devlin knew he should have told her the truth, at least before they'd left for the station. The moment he kissed her that morning he'd been certain she didn't remember what had happened the night before. If he knew women at all, and he did, Gabrielle was driving herself crazy trying to figure out whether they'd actually slept together.

A decent man would have told her, but Devlin never claimed to be decent. Which was why his nobility the evening before hadn't set well with him. It smacked of weakness and that made him uneasy. No, uneasy wasn't the word. It irritated the hell out of him. He had wanted to get to her, because *she'd* gotten to him, so he'd let the charade play on. But it was beginning to leave a bad taste in his mouth.

As they walked down the narrow third-floor hallway he glanced at her. Her face was still pale and her lips were stretched into a tight, thin line, as though she were in pain. Hell, she probably was, he thought. Her hangover must be a doozy.

He watched her hand come up and clutch spasmodically at her chest. Sweat beaded on her forehead, and she grew even paler. A doozy, all right. Low blow, Sinclair, he told himself, ashamed for taking advantage of her when she was down. To steady her, he put his hand beneath her arm. "Where's the rest room? Can you make it there?"

Her eyes were opened wide, the pure panic in them sending off palpable waves of anxiety. "Yes— no—I'm—" Gasping, she tried again. "I'm—fine."

Her chest rose and fell rapidly. No way would she make it far, he thought. He looked around for options, but before he could decide what to do, she solved the problem by dashing into the stairwell. Devlin figured there were worse places and followed her.

She was crouched down against the wall of the stairwell. After another look of horror and a desperate, "Go away!" which he ignored, she started ripping through her purse, frantically searching for something. Devlin couldn't imagine what she wanted, but it occurred to him that if she'd been about to throw up, she'd already held off longer than he'd have thought possible. Pills? he wondered. Was she looking for medicine of some sort?

He squatted and grabbed the purse from her, dumping the contents out and spreading them over the floor. Junk. Keys, mints, lipstick, a novel, notes. Pens, a checkbook, a wallet. And there it was, bright as a beacon even before she snatched it up. A plain brown paper bag, carefully folded.

You could've blown him over with a gentle breeze. A panic attack? he wondered, staring as she fit the open end of the bag over her mouth. Damn straight, and a monster one, at that. She huddled against the wall, breathing in and out of the paper bag. Devlin helped her sit, then sat beside her. Gently, he pushed her head down, unconsciously stroking her hair, patting her back, murmuring soothing sounds.

As he waited for her to regain control, his emotions reeled in total chaos. He had seen one or two people hyperventilate before, but he'd never seen the equal of Gabrielle's attack. Gabrielle Rousseau, subject to blowout panic attacks? Of all people he would never have suspected to have such a problem, Gabrielle topped the list. Yet he was seeing it with his own eyes.

He didn't know how much time had passed when she finally dropped her hands to her lap and leaned her head back against the wall. From above, Devlin heard a door open, and a few seconds later a policeman clattered down the stairs.

"Everything all right here?" he asked, giving them a sharp-eyed look as he paused at the landing.

"Fine," Devlin said. "My associate just had a dizzy spell. Touch of flu, I guess." With a nod, the officer continued on his way.

"Thanks."

Her voice was so low and strained, Devlin barely heard the word. "Better now?" he asked, smoothing her hair back from her face. The tender gesture surprised him as much as it apparently did Gabrielle. Good God, what was happening here? What he felt went beyond mere compassion. He wanted to . . . protect her, he realized. Shield her. And he wasn't at all sure he could deal with that feeling.

Her eyes wide, the pupils dilated, she stared at him and slowly nodded. "They don't last long."

"Do you have these often?"

"No." She spoke quickly, too quickly. Closing her eyes, she was silent for a few moments. "I'm all right," she said, taking another deep breath. "Let's go."

Devlin rose and helped her up. If she had the attacks so rarely, why did she carry a paper bag in her purse? He waited until they were in the parking lot before he said, "Have you seen a doctor about this?"

Her back stiffened; her chin lifted. He watched the transformation from shaky and weak to strong and in control with admiration and not a little awe.

But it only reinforced his certainty that Gabrielle was no stranger to these attacks.

"No. I told you, this doesn't happen often." She glared a challenge at him while waiting for him to unlock the car door.

He met her gaze with a look of patent disbelief. "Right. If you say so."

"It's just an aberration," she snapped. "Like what happened between us last night."

NINE

Damn, he hadn't seen that one coming, Devlin thought, admiring her tactics. Attack and distract. Exactly what he did when he felt threatened or showed a weakness.

"An aberration," he said, his gaze running shrewdly over her. "Which means that you don't think what happened last night will ever happen again."

Her nose lifted arrogantly in the air. "Very sharp, Sinclair. Now I see why you're such a wonder in the courtroom." Her tone was dry, sarcastic, and pitched to irritate him to the max.

If they really had made love the night before, he'd be mad as the devil right now, he thought. As it was, he could guarantee that the same scenario wouldn't occur again. Because next time he had Gabrielle naked in a bed with him, she would be stone-cold sober and they'd damn sure finish what they'd started.

He cranked the engine and turned on the air conditioner, allowing Gabrielle to think she'd gotten in the last word. Knowing there was no faster, surer way to infuriate a woman than by not responding when she expected it, he kept silent during the short drive to Alfonso's. By the time he pulled into the parking lot he could feel the frustration steaming from her. He admitted he was being a jerk by baiting her, but he found an angry Gabrielle infinitely easier to deal with than the woman who'd touched his heart and stirred his compassion in the dirty stairwell of the police station.

He drove up beside her car and parked. "Not so fast, sweetheart," he said, halting her escape by grabbing hold of her wrist. "Exactly what are you saying won't happen again?"

"Don't play stupid. You know what I'm talking about," she said, her eyes flashing bright with anger.

"Spell it out for me."

"S-e-x." She tossed her head back and raised her chin in challenge. "Last night was an impulse, and it's not going to happen again. Get it now?"

"Oh, I get it," he said, nodding. "You're saying you won't be making those sweet little sounds you made when I sucked on your neck. That spot right at the hollow, where you're so sensitive."

"No," she said between gritted teeth. "I won't."

"And you won't be clawing my back with your nails at the same time you're making those sounds."

"I didn't—" she started to protest. Glaring at him, she continued, "Not that either."

"What about all those things you were whispering in my ear? The things you were promising to do to me and the things you wanted me to do to you? You won't be doing that again either?"

Anger rolled off her in waves, raising the temperature in the car by several degrees. She started to speak, but Devlin continued, lowering his voice to a seductive murmur. "And what about how you screamed when you ca—"

"None of it!" she shouted. "We're not doing any of it again!"

"Well, that's certainly clear," he said. "But," he added with an indulgent smile, "I'm afraid you're the one who doesn't get it. There's a little detail you don't seem to be aware of." He pulled her closer until his lips were just a few inches from hers and said softly, "None of it ever happened."

Shock widened her eyes, deepening their color to a murky green. He was a prime bastard for treating her so badly, but it was better she find that out about him now instead of later when it would only hurt her more.

"Wh–what?"

"Well, that's not quite true," he said, considering. "Some of it happened. But the main event didn't. You see, sweetheart, we didn't make love last night."

"We d–didn't?" she whispered.

"Afraid not." His gaze flickered over her as he allowed silence to dominate. With one hand, he tilted up her chin. "I like my lovers conscious."

Cruel but necessary, he told himself, seeing the hurt dawn in her eyes. He wanted her, but he didn't intend for her to harbor any illusions. His ambitions didn't include being destroyed the way his father had been or being made a fool of again like Celine had done. Gabrielle deserved to know what she'd be getting if she chose to go to bed with him.

At the moment she looked much more interested in strangling him than sleeping with him. She'd lost the hurt look completely. Her face reddened, her eyes narrowed, and she jerked her wrist out of his grasp with a furious twist. Her wrathful gaze locked with his and held for a long, turbulent minute.

Then she slugged him.

No gentle tap, but a right to his jaw that snapped his head back, made his eyes water, and had him worrying she'd loosened a couple of his teeth. A slap would have been expected, but the punch shocked the hell out of him. But then, Gabrielle never did what he expected. Gingerly, he put his hand on his jaw and wiggled it before deciding it wasn't broken.

"So much for chivalry," he said. "You slugged me for not taking advantage of you when you were drunk?"

"No, I slugged you because you strung me along when you knew I didn't remember what had happened. And you're damned lucky that's all I did." She got out of the car, then leaned down to speak to him. "Thanks for a forgettable evening, *darling*," she said, and slammed the door shut with window-rattling force.

Devlin watched her drive off, wondering if he'd finally outsmarted himself. Not exactly his usual smooth handling of a woman. He seemed to act like a SOB a lot around Gabrielle, and he liked it less each time it happened.

Gabrielle stirred up unwanted feelings, unacknowledged dreams that he hadn't felt or been in touch with in a decade. His response to her scared the hell out of him. No other woman—with the exception of a select few of his clients—had ever roused his protective instincts to the degree Gabrielle did. No other woman had roused any of the feelings that had bombarded him last night and today. Oh hell, admit it, he thought. She'd been stirring him up since the day he met her. Making him feel, making him want, making him hunger for things he knew didn't exist. Making him . . . weak.

A bad sign in a man who didn't believe he had a heart or a conscience.

Music supposedly soothed the savage beast, but right now it wasn't doing that for Gabrielle. She'd reached home in such a turmoil that she could barely think. Instead of rehashing an impossible situation, she'd turned to her major solace of the last fifteen years. Her piano.

Beginning with a particularly violent piece by Saint-Saëns, she ripped through, in rapid succession, selections of Bach, Beethoven, and Mozart suited to her present vindictive mood. With each passionate, haunting note she vented her anger, her humiliation, and finally, a very small portion of her despair. As the last direful, lingering notes of Beethoven's "Pathétique Sonata" echoed in the air, her fingers faltered at the keyboard. No matter how much she focused her anger on Devlin, and on herself for her stupidity in falling for him in the first place, she knew she was avoiding the worst problem.

Her eyes closed and her head bowed, touching the keyboard with a discordant note of hopelessness. How could she do it? How could she reconcile having the means to successfully defend her client and yet deliberately withhold the evidence? Doing so meant compromising her career, her belief in the law, her ethics. And look what had happened already; she'd had a panic attack in front of Devlin. She'd handed him a lovely weapon to wield against her, and she didn't doubt he'd make superb use of it.

Yet what would happen if she didn't hide that report? Getting Franco off would solve none of her problems, except her moral dilemma. Because Franco wouldn't fade away once he was free. He'd hang around, a dark, malicious albatross, until he totally destroyed her life. Again.

She closed the keyboard cover on another dream that had died. No amount of agonizing would change the bottom line. If she followed through with her impulse and hid the police report, if she didn't use every means at her disposal to gain her client's acquittal, then she truly was no better than Franco. She might as well have stayed under Vito's control and lived the life of the Mafia princess she'd been born to. Everything she'd done for the last fourteen years would have been in vain. Her whole way of life would be a mockery.

How could doing the right thing feel so wrong? She had no other choice but to expose the police error, and consequently, enable Franco Sabatino to go free.

Rocky, lying stretched out beside the piano, raised her head and stared at the front door. A few seconds later a knock sounded. The dog rushed to the door and scratched at it, whining happily, her tail wagging. At least the visitor wasn't Franco, Gabrielle thought.

She crossed the living room to look out the

peephole. Devlin. How dare he show his face there after the number he'd pulled on her? She didn't answer, but folded her arms over her chest and waited to see what he'd do.

"Gabrielle," he called, pounding on the door this time. "I know you're in there. I heard you playing."

She stuck her tongue out, feeling better after the childish action. More pounding. Rocky scratched at the door again and looked at her expectantly. Dumb dog didn't realize that Devlin was as big a threat as Franco.

"Dammit, Gabrielle, let me in," he shouted, his voice muffled by the barrier. "I need to talk to you."

"Go to hell!" she shouted right back. "And get off my property before I call the police." Not that she'd carry things so far, but he didn't need to know that. She waited, Rocky whining beside her, but didn't hear any more noise. Minutes passed with no other sounds. Had he actually left?

The sound of glass shattering had her whirling around and rushing to her bedroom. By the time she and Rocky reached it, Devlin had pushed up the window and was already halfway inside. Stunned by the sight of the urbane, sophisticated Devlin Sinclair crawling through her broken bedroom window and swearing a blue streak as he did so, Gabrielle could only gape.

Rocky launched herself at him, but from the

furious wagging of her tail Gabrielle suspected the attack would be more on the order of licking him to death. Brushing glass shards from his shirt and jeans, Devlin quelled the dog's enthusiasm with a word. Rocky promptly sat on her haunches, panting and gazing at him adoringly.

"You should put her out before she cuts herself," he said.

Parking her fists on her hips, Gabrielle found her voice. "I don't believe this." She glared at him, wishing she had something to throw. "What the hell do you think you're doing?"

He shrugged. "I needed to talk to you, and it was obvious you weren't going to let me in."

"Gee, I wonder why?" she said sarcastically. "Could it be because I've had enough humiliation for one day?"

A flush rose in his cheeks. Gabrielle decided she must be dreaming. Devlin Sinclair, blushing?

"That's what—I didn't mean—" He broke off, grinding his teeth and swearing savagely under his breath. "Dammit, this is harder than I thought it would be. I came here to apologize."

"Are you apologizing for not taking advantage of me, as you put it, or for letting me think you did?"

His jawline hardened. "For letting you think we'd made love. For telling you like I did. For—" He broke off again, grimacing. "For being such a bastard when I did tell you the truth."

Gabrielle had the feeling Devlin didn't often apologize for his words or actions. Privately, she admitted that he had reason to be angry, or at least frustrated, about the night before. Besides that, she knew quite a few men who wouldn't have cared what condition she'd been in.

Well, so what? she thought. That didn't say a lot about the men she knew, and it didn't justify Devlin stringing her along like he had. She couldn't forgive and forget quite so easily. And if that wasn't enough, he'd witnessed her panic attack as well.

Why didn't he just go away and leave her to her misery? "Okay, you've apologized. You've admitted you were a jerk, and I'll admit I was a fool to drink so much. Can we just forget it now?"

He shook his head, smiling ruefully. "Unfortunately, no, I can't forget it. I wish to hell I could."

So did she. Gabrielle felt her throat close and tears sting her eyes. Why wouldn't he go away? Hadn't she made a fool of herself enough times already? Abruptly, she said, "Rocky, come. Time to go out." Turning on her heel, she left the room.

He followed her, of course. She sensed his presence behind her as she stood in the open doorway to the backyard and wished desperately that she didn't care what Devlin thought of her, or how he felt about her. Wished desperately that she only knew the face he showed the rest of the world and not the one he hid. The man who had so generously helped Marcie Field. The man who'd comforted her in a dingy stairwell. That man existed, no matter how much Devlin tried to deny it.

His hands fell on her shoulders, warm, strong, gentle. "You make me feel things I don't want to feel," he said, his voice low, quiet. "And I don't like it."

Her back still toward him, she said, "You wanted to make me angry and you succeeded. Why?" She felt his cheek against her hair, the warmth of his solid body against her back.

He kneaded her shoulders. "I told myself I wanted you to know what kind of man I am. To understand that I can't offer you more than sex. To establish the rules so you wouldn't get hurt."

His warm breath wafted across her ear, her cheek. It shouldn't have been seductive, but it was. "Did you think me so naive, I didn't know that?" She turned to look him in the face and search his eyes. "I think you wanted to make me so mad, I'd never go to bed with you. Are you going to tell me why?"

He stared at her for a long time. He didn't look angry; he looked confused, unsure of himself. It wasn't a look she'd ever have associated with his face, or emotions she would ever have expected him to have.

He turned his back to her and strode quickly from the room, swearing under his breath again. Gabrielle closed the back door and followed him, understanding less of what was happening with each passing moment.

"That's it, isn't it?" she asked. "You wanted to make sure we'd never make love. But you've been trying to get me in bed since we met. Why the sudden turnaround?"

Grimacing, he shoved his hands through his hair, the gold strands falling back in disorder. "I don't believe this," he muttered, and sat on the sofa.

She crossed the room to stand in front of him. "You're not making sense."

"Tell me about it." He looked up at her. "Yeah, you're right. I said it to tick you off. Subconsciously, I wanted to drive you as far away from me as possible."

Confused, Gabrielle frowned and stared down at him. "All you had to do was quit making moves on me. You didn't have to—" She hesitated as she remembered essentially throwing herself at him. Flushing, she continued, "If you weren't interested, you didn't have to drive me home last night."

He made a sound halfway between a groan and a laugh. "I've wanted to make love to you since you dropped that lingerie at my feet, Gabrielle. And when I want something, I usually get it. But then last night and today, I finally figured something out." His gaze connected with hers, his eyes dark gray, unhappy. "You're different. I'm different. This whole thing between us is different."

It wasn't getting any clearer. Tired, bewildered, her emotions dangerously unstable, she needed for him to stop speaking in riddles. "Devlin, what in the world are you talking about? Spit it out."

His jaw tightened. "Dammit, Gabrielle, I think I'm in love with you."

TEN

"Excuse me?" Gabrielle said. In love with her? Devlin was in love with her? Staring down at him, she stifled the urge to knock her hand against her ear. "Say that again."

He shot her a dirty look. "You heard me. I said I think I'm in love with you."

Her heart pounded hard. He couldn't mean it, could he? "You *think* you're in love with me? What, are you hoping it will pass, like a bad cold?"

His lips twitched. "All right. I'm in love with you."

Maybe the alcohol hadn't left her system and she was having a flashback, Gabrielle thought, still staring at him.

"God, I can't believe I just told you that," he muttered, more to himself than to her. He blew out his breath on a long sigh and shoved a hand through his hair again. "Surprised the hell out of me too."

Why would he tell her he loved her? What kind of cruel game was he playing now? The longer she looked at him and thought about it, the stronger her fury grew. Her chest heaving with emotion, she launched herself at him, intent on inflicting pain. "You pig! Jerk! Do you think I'll fall for this line? I don't know what kind of game you—"

Before she could connect, he grabbed both of her wrists and wrestled her down. She landed on her back on the couch, her legs splayed across his lap. He glared at her while she struggled. "Dammit, Gabrielle, stop it! I'm not playing games. It's the truth."

Unable to break his iron grip, she stilled and stared up into his face. Even angry, she couldn't deny he got to her. He seemed serious, and not happy about the matter, either. Besides, Devlin wasn't the type to profess love just to get a woman into bed. He didn't need to, and he knew it.

Maybe he did mean it. Devlin Sinclair, the eternal Don Juan, had just told her he was in love with her. This had to be a dream. "Why?" she whispered.

"Why am I in love with you?"

She nodded.

For the first time since he started the conversation, Devlin smiled. That take-off-your-clothes-and-I-promise-to-make-you-a-happy-woman smile.

But for some reason, it looked like he was smiling just for her. Her bones turned to cream cheese, and her heart gave a funny lurch. Oh, God, no. She couldn't be in love with him too. Could she?

His gaze ran down her body while he considered her, returning to her eyes after a long study. "I think it's your mouth." She blinked. He shifted his grip to hold her wrists together, still stretched above her head. Slowly, he traced his forefinger over her lips, barely touching them. "Smart. Sassy." Smiling, he dipped his finger inside her mouth and continued tracing with the finger now dampened. Gabrielle had never felt anything quite like it in her life. Her stomach fluttered, her breasts tightened, her skin tingled. All from the touch of his finger tracing her lips. And the look in his eyes as he did so.

"Quick," he added, his voice deepening. "And then there's how your mouth looks. Soft, wide, beautiful. Tempting." While he spoke, he continued the mesmerizing motion of his finger, sliding it into her mouth, taking it out and shaping her lips.

Gabrielle couldn't have spoken if the couch had caught on fire. He was too smooth, too gorgeous, too knowing to be for real, but oh, she didn't care. If he didn't kiss her soon, she was going to explode.

"But the best thing," he murmured, his voice a husky caress, "is how you taste. Warm." He kissed a corner of her mouth, as lightly as an imaginary lover might have. "Giving." He repeated the caress at the other corner. "Seductive." For an instant only, he touched his lips to hers, then drew back to stare at her once again.

Spellbound, Gabrielle could barely breathe. The only thought she had was to wish he would kiss her, really kiss her, and end the torture. Except she knew that would be only the beginning.

"Sweet," he whispered, his mouth coming closer, hovering a breath away. "So damn sweet," he said, then he kissed her and she went up in flames.

His tongue stroked inside, touched and toyed with hers, slipped out and in again to repeat the tantalizing process. Eager to touch, to caress his chest, she whimpered against his mouth and tried to free her arms. He held her still, deepening the kiss until she felt as fluid as water.

Finally, he released her arms, and she wrapped them around his neck, pulling him closer. His lips blazed a wet, heated trail down her neck, and she arched it to offer him better access. His teeth scraped at the hollow, then he pressed his open mouth against her throat, making her shiver, making her burn.

Her mind shouted that she was flirting with disaster, playing with a more dangerous fire than she could imagine, but she had never felt this strong, this alive, so she ignored it. She didn't want to think. In the morning she would think. Tonight . . . tonight was for emotions, and she gave herself freely to the erotic sensations buffeting her.

Shifting their position, Devlin lay almost fully

on top of her, the weight of his body a seduction in itself, and her legs parted to hold him intimately against her. It had been so long since she'd felt a man's heavy weight, felt a man's desire for her.

He lifted his head and gazed at her. "Tell me no, Gabrielle. Stop me now, or I won't stop until I'm so deep inside you that neither of us will be able to think or breathe."

Her heart somersaulted, and Gabrielle knew if she hadn't been lost before, she was now. The hard ridge of his arousal pressed at the softness of her thighs, a promise of passion still to come. She breathed in his scent, and her senses swam with longing. He wanted her to *stop* him? Nothing short of an atom bomb would stop them from making love this time.

She didn't trust herself to speak, but worked his knit shirt from his jeans, her eyes never leaving his. He sat back as she rose, until they were side by side on the couch and his shirttail hung free. Her hands slipped underneath, gliding over the bare skin of his chest as she pushed the shirt higher, until she had stripped him of it. Her breath caught deep in her throat as she stared at him.

His shoulders were broad, his arms and his chest well-toned but not bulky. Underneath the smooth golden tanned skin, his muscles rippled as she spread her hands over his chest in a wonder of discovery. A light sprinkling of blond hair ran down the center of his chest, growing heavier the lower her gaze reached, until it disappeared under the waistband of his jeans. Though she'd guessed that his clothes hid a beautiful body, she hadn't known just how intoxicating that bare expanse of flesh stretched taut over muscle and sinew would be until she saw it. Until she touched the warm, naked skin and felt him quiver in response to her.

They stared at each other in silence, then she guided his hands underneath her top, halting only when they covered her breasts. "Make love with me, Devlin," she said, wondering if that could really be her voice sounding so husky, so inviting.

His eyes flared bright with passion. He pushed her top up, stripping her as she had stripped him moments earlier. As he gazed at her breasts, covered by a white French bra made mostly of lace, he smiled, a slow, wicked smile of promise.

"Pretty," he said, and flicked the bra open with a deft twist of his wrist. Spreading the wisps of fabric, he covered her breasts with warm palms, and she gasped at the exquisite feel of his hands on her bare skin. "But these"—he squeezed her breasts gently and rubbed his palms over her nipples—"are beautiful." Then he bent his head and fastened his mouth over one taut crest.

Fiery shivers of sensation shot from her breast to the heat pooling between her legs. Her back arched, and her head fell back. She buried her fingers in the thick, silky strands of his hair and clung to him. His mouth clamped hard on her other nipple, then he rolled his tongue around it, taunting, teasing while he bore her down onto the couch. He continued to torment her, alternately sucking her nipples and laving her breasts with warm moisture. Her blood hummed, spreading the sweet agony to every part of her body. His hand slid between her thighs and cupped her through her jeans. Her hips jerked, and she gave a strangled groan when he unzipped her pants and worked his hand inside the denim to caress her through her satin panties.

Muttering something—a curse, a prayer—Devlin shoved the narrow strip of satin aside and stroked his fingers over her bare flesh. "God." He groaned. "You feel like heaven." Another stroke, then he thrust his finger inside her, slid out, and thrust inside again. "Sweet, hot heaven."

Her muscles clenched, tightening around his finger. Was it possible to die from pleasure? She saw him watching her. Watching the movements of his hand and her reaction to him. She couldn't help but lift her hips and moan his name in supplication.

"Let go, Gabrielle. I want to see you."

His words as much as the tormenting action of his thumb on her center of pleasure sent her spiraling. Even if she'd wanted to, she couldn't have halted the release that swept over her like heat shimmering in the desert. He gave her no time to recover, but continued the blissful torture until he'd pushed her to the brink again. "Devlin, I want you now," she said, choking off the last word when he slipped another finger inside her.

"Shh," he said, kissing her mouth while he continued the motions of his hand. "Slow down."

"I can't. Now. I want you now," she whispered, and placed her hand over his erection. Boldly, she caressed him, but soon the denim interfered with her exploration. She tore open the button of his jeans eagerly, but the strength of his arousal forced her to go much more slowly when she lowered his zipper.

He covered her hand, pressing it against him for a moment before he groaned and moved it away. "Later," he said, hooking his hands in her jeans and jerking them down, along with her panties. "We'll go slow later." He stood and shoved his own jeans down over his hips while she watched, sprawled on the couch and feeling more wanton than she ever imagined.

When he stood naked before her she whispered, "Oh, Lord," and stretched out a hand to touch him. He smiled, but as she stroked him, her caresses growing bolder, his expression tightened. Impatiently, he brushed her hands aside to lie between her thighs, his sex warm and heavy against hers. He took her face between his hands and gazed into her eyes, then kissed her deeply, his tongue mimicking the slow, rocking rhythm of his hips against hers. Long moments later, he heaved a tortured groan, and she felt him shift. His hand dropped away from her face to dangle off the couch.

"What's wrong?" Was that her voice? That breathless, achy sound?

"Nothing. If I can just find—" He stretched his

arm farther back just as she rose to see what he was doing, and they tumbled onto the rug with a thud.

"Damn!" Devlin swore.

"What happened?" Lucky for her, she'd landed on top of him. His stifled groan made her wonder if he'd smacked his head against the table, or it could have been her elbow that had landed in his stomach.

"We fell off the couch." Moving her aside, he grabbed his jeans and pulled his wallet from the hip pocket. "Here." He handed her a foil packet and glared at the coffee table butting up against them. "This has got to go," he said, and shoved it back several feet. It teetered, the glass top shaking, but then settled into place without turning over.

Gabrielle bit the inside of her cheek to keep from giggling and fumbled with the condom. Her fingers wouldn't cooperate, and she looked up at him apologetically. "I can't get it—"

He grabbed the small package from her and ripped it open. "I can," he said, and took care of it while his smoldering gaze lingered on her body like a touch.

Suddenly shy, Gabrielle closed her legs together. It was crazy, after what they'd been doing to each other leading to this moment, but actually making love seemed such a final step.

"Hey," he said softly, kneeling beside her. "Change your mind?" His large, warm hand slipped between her legs, gently urging them apart.

He waited, his hand covering her, caressing the core of her desire.

"Um—" She could hardly breathe, let alone talk. "No."

"Good," he said, and kissed her.

Seconds later, his shaft pressed against her heated flesh, against the ache raging within, then he slid into her slowly, letting her feel each spectacular inch of his entry until he was imbedded deeply inside her. He buried his face in her neck, and she heard his ragged breathing, felt the tenseness of his muscles as he waited for her to adjust to him. A tenderness she couldn't explain stole over her, and she wrapped her arms tighter around him, fighting the emotion that threatened to engulf her.

He pulled out of her, waited a heart-stopping beat, and surged back inside. Gabrielle dug her nails into his back, lifting her hips to meet his and tightening her legs around him. The tempo of his thrusts quickened, then slowed, then quickened again until she felt the storm peak, the moment before all hell, or heaven, breaks loose. Wave after wave of excitement swept her up, tumbling her over and over, then her climax rolled through her hard, fast, and shattering. Devlin moaned her name. His name broke on her sigh. His release shuddered through him as he spent himself deep inside her. Lost in love, she held tight while their last tremors died away.

❦———————❦

Exactly when had he lost his mind? Devlin wondered some time later. They lay on the rug, too lazy to move, with Gabrielle snuggled in the curve of his arm. He was spent, satisfied, and dammit, he wanted her again. Every moment they made love he'd been intensely aware that it was Gabrielle he held, Gabrielle he kissed, Gabrielle who responded so ardently to his touch. Gabrielle who touched him, kissed him, made love to him. It hadn't been just fantastic sex. It had been fantastic because it was Gabrielle.

What lunacy had come over him? He'd not only committed the ultimate folly of falling in love with her, but he'd *told* her about it. Opened his mouth and let out the riskiest confession of his life. Devlin knew what women did with that kind of knowledge. They used it, and God help the man who gave them the edge.

He looked down at her hand resting trustingly on his chest. She wasn't like that, he thought, caressing her bare back and hip. Or was that just wishful thinking?

She chose that moment to raise up on her elbow and look at him. "Regrets?" she asked softly.

Her dark hair hung down, the ends brushing against his chest with a soft, ticklish feeling. Her lips were swollen from his kisses, her eyes slumberous. She looked like a woman who'd just been well loved. And she was so beautiful, it almost hurt him to look at her. "I think that's my line," he said huskily. "But no. No regrets."

"You look awfully serious."

He picked up her hand and kissed each knuckle. God, he had it bad. "What about you?"

Her eyes softened even more. She seemed as bemused as he was. "No." She shook her head. "No regrets."

"Good." He slid his hand through her hair to the back of her head, bringing her mouth down to his. "Because I want you again." He kissed her, pulling her naked body on top of his, and she flowed over him like a sigh, a whisper, a dream.

ELEVEN

At midnight Gabrielle stood in front of the refrigerator, trying to scrounge up something edible. Her choices were limited. A limp head of lettuce. Some sort of sauce in a covered dish. Either spaghetti sauce from a couple of weeks ago or . . . No, she thought shuddering, surely she'd cleaned out the refrigerator since then. At least the milk was in date. She figured that as long as she had milk, coffee, and bread, she wouldn't starve.

Grocery shopping hadn't been high on her list lately. Besides, she hadn't expected company. Or anything else that had happened that night, either. A foolish grin tugged at her mouth. She touched her fingers to her still-swollen lips and sighed.

"Find anything?" Devlin asked from behind her, his arms slipping around her waist. He nuzzled her ear. "I'll admit"—he bit her ear gently—

"you're great to nibble on, but it doesn't do much to fill my stomach."

She laughed. "We had a deal, remember? I find the food and you clean up the mess. You couldn't have done it already." She'd been very careful not to mention she couldn't cook worth beans.

"I'm a wonder with a vacuum," he said, pushing her robe aside and kissing her neck. "Call the glass man Monday and have him replace the window and send me the bill."

"Don't think I won't," she told him, but she turned in his arms to kiss him. "I thought you were hungry," she murmured when his hands slid over her rear.

"I am, but you're distracting me."

She sighed and gestured at the shelves. "I don't have much here. Eggs, milk, and bread."

"Omelette," Devlin said, peering inside. "Got any vegetables or cheese?"

"Vegetables?" Dubiously, she looked into the refrigerator, then back at him. "Are you sure you want an omelette?"

His lips twitched. "Okay, no omelette. How about powdered sugar?" She shook her head. "Maple syrup?"

"Yes," she said, confused. "To make what?"

"French toast."

Might as well come clean, she thought. "I can't make French toast. Or omelettes either. Scrambled eggs is pretty much my limit. I don't cook much."

He grinned at her. "I sort of suspected that. That's all right, I'll cook."

His proficiency didn't surprise her as much as his obvious enjoyment of the process. Gabrielle considered cooking a form of torture. Almost anything else, in her viewpoint, beat cooking. "This is great," she told him, sopping up syrup with another melt-in-your-mouth bite of French toast. "How did you learn to cook? Did your mother teach you?"

He gave a caustic laugh. "My mother wouldn't be caught dead in a kitchen. Except to tell the cook what to prepare."

Touched a nerve there, she thought. "Your family had a cook?"

He hunched a shoulder and took a bite of food. "Several. In succession. My mother liked to fire the help on a regular basis."

That he came from a well-to-do family didn't surprise her, but the bitterness in his voice did. "So who taught you? The cook?" He shook his head. "A girlfriend?" Imagining that, jealousy hit her like a slap in the face. There was no point at all in thinking about the women in Devlin's past. She'd drive herself insane if she did.

He shook his head again and smiled. "I taught myself. When I got out of law school I didn't have much money. It was learn to cook cheaply or starve."

"But your family—" She broke off, seeing the sardonic expression on his face. Old, unhealed wounds, judging by his reaction. "I'm sorry. I don't mean to pry."

"No, that's okay." He covered her hand and squeezed it. "I'm not used to talking to anyone about my family. I don't think about them much if I can help it."

"Then forget I said anything," she said, realizing she'd better steer the conversation away from family. What if he asked about hers? She couldn't tell him the truth, had never been able to tell anyone, which was why every relationship she'd had since she left home hadn't worked. Would this time be different? Could she ever tell Devlin the truth?

He continued as if he hadn't heard her. "My parents disowned me when I went to work with the public defender's office."

"Why?" she blurted out, stunned.

His mouth curved in a thin smile. "My mother thought it was tacky. Sinclairs didn't *do* that sort of thing. Especially not Lydia and Preston Sinclair's only offspring. She had grandiose plans for me to practice corporate law."

Gabrielle knew she ought to shut up, but she couldn't help wanting to know more about yet another side to Devlin she hadn't suspected. "What about your father?"

Devlin shrugged. "My father never stood up for himself. Why would he have stood up for me?"

She wanted to hold him, soothe the hurt away, but she wasn't sure he'd accept it. And she sensed she was getting into dangerous territory. "Are you still estranged from them?"

Tapping his fork against his water glass, he nodded. "My father's dead. When Lydia heard I'd joined CG and S, she decided maybe I was worthy of being her son after all. She still makes periodic attempts to drag me back into the fold, even though she realizes by now that it's useless."

He stood and pulled Gabrielle to her feet. "So," he said, drawing her close, "what about your deep, dark secrets?"

Even though she'd expected the question, it wasn't easy to answer him nonchalantly. "Unless you want to know that I had a crush on my high school science teacher in the ninth grade, I'm afraid I don't have any."

"A woman without secrets." He kissed her neck and murmured, "I've never met one before."

Her heart constricted. Here was the perfect opportunity to rectify her omission. To follow her conscience, do the right thing, even though it was a little late. "Devlin, about today . . ." Her voice trailed off. It was hard to concentrate when he was nuzzling along her collarbone. "I might have missed something in those police reports."

"Okay," he said. Clearly uninterested in the topic, he traced his tongue across her skin.

"No, listen." She pushed at him, and he drew back, giving her a long-suffering expression.

"Do we have to talk about work right now?"

"Yes. I've been thinking about it, and I might

have missed something. I wasn't feeling very well, you know."

His eyes darkened as he looked at her. "Yeah, I remember. Your panic attack. Are you ready to tell me what brought it on?"

"If I knew, I'd tell you." She willed herself to meet his gaze unflinchingly.

He didn't look convinced, and his words bore it out. "Would you?"

"Of course I would." It sounded weak, even to her, but she plowed on. "By the time I reached the last couple of reports, I'd started feeling bad. So I think we should go over them again."

"All right. Monday we'll do it. Tomorrow I've got other plans."

Disappointment stabbed through her. "You don't need to go. I'll handle it myself," she said, trying not to sound hurt.

His smile was slow and sexy. "That would be a shame. I had an idea"—he parted her robe, sliding it off her shoulders and down her arms—"involving you and me"—he cupped her breasts as the robe pooled around her feet—"and a lot of time. It goes something like this." His head bent, and he traced his tongue around her nipple, through the lacy fabric of her gown. She was wearing the black negligee Devlin had said he'd found the night before and dreamed about taking off her. Naturally, after a confession like that she couldn't resist putting it on.

"Well . . ." She groaned as his mouth taunted

one breast and his hand the other. "When you put it that way . . ."

He backed her up against the door and gathered the nightgown in his hands, slowly pushing it up her legs as he knelt in front of her.

Realizing they weren't going to make it to the bedroom, she started to say, "Don't we need—?"

"Don't worry," he murmured, his breath warm against her skin. "I've got it covered."

Her laugh turned to a sigh of pleasure as he placed his mouth at the apex of her thighs. And then she didn't think at all for a very long time.

Later, they lay in her bed with his arm curved around her and her head on his chest, while he idly stroked her waist and hip. "Did you plan this tonight?" she asked.

In the light cast from the hallway she saw him smile. "Making love? Not exactly. But I told you I've wanted you since I met you."

"Do you always carry a box of condoms around in your car?" The question had been nagging at her since they'd used the two in his wallet and he'd gone to his car for more. She wanted to be the only woman in his bed. Was she?

He looked down at her. "In case I get lucky, you mean?" he asked, a slow grin stealing over his face. "What's wrong, sweetheart? Jealous?"

"Insanely," she said, not sure what had made her answer him truthfully.

His grin faded, replaced by a tender smile. "You're really something," he said, and kissed her lips. "That box is a memento of an affair that never happened. Do you want to know why it never happened?"

She nodded, mesmerized by his eyes and the seductive sound of his voice.

"Because I met you. And I haven't thought about another woman since I first laid eyes on you. That should have been my first clue that you were different and I was in deep trouble."

"You're very good," she whispered.

His gaze, dark gray and intense, held hers captive. "This isn't a line, Gabrielle. I think I fell for you the first time I saw you."

Her heart lurched. She broke eye contact and tried to cover her emotions with a light laugh. "Right. The klutz who landed at your feet in a lingerie shop. You don't seem the type to believe in love at first sight."

"I'm not. In fact, I didn't believe in love, period. Not since—" He broke off and looked at her.

A woman, Gabrielle thought, and wondered how badly he'd been hurt. She desperately wanted to know, to know everything that had shaped him, had made him who he was. But she had no right to ask, so she remained silent.

He brushed her cheek with his fingertips, laid his fingers lightly on her lips. "There are a lot of things I haven't believed in for a long time. But you've changed that."

She gazed into his eyes, filled with passion and promise, and believed him. As crazy, as improbable as it seemed, she believed he loved her. Guilt crushed her heart like a vise. God, she wanted so much to tell him about her past. But she was a coward. She was afraid to see that loving look in his eyes turn to disgust. Disgust for who she was. For the lie she'd lived for fourteen years. The lie she would continue to live.

Instead she put her arms around his neck and whispered, "Kiss me, Devlin."

His mouth against hers was as tender and loving as a dream, and the night bled into dawn.

"Damn," Devlin muttered, as he nicked himself while shaving the next morning. What in the hell was wrong with the dog? Rocky's frantic barking and growling were ear-splitting, even in the bathroom with the door closed. He scraped the last of his beard off, rinsed Gabrielle's razor, and reached for a towel, slinging it around his neck.

"Get out!" he heard Gabrielle shout as he walked into the living room. She had her hands wrapped around Rocky's collar and was straining to hold her back. "I told you not—"

"Call off the dog," Franco Sabatino said. "Call the damned thing off or I'll gut it."

Devlin halted at the hall doorway and stared. Sabatino? What the hell was he doing there? Gabrielle continued to struggle with Rocky, who lunged at the intruder, slavering, teeth bared and out for blood, as vicious as any junkyard mongrel.

He couldn't believe this was the same dog who'd welcomed him with tail-wagging adoration the night before, when he'd broken into Gabrielle's house.

The rest of their words were drowned out in the furious cacophony the dog set up, but he saw Sabatino reach inside his jacket. Devlin was already moving toward him when the sun bounced a ray off hard steel. Six inches long and gleaming wickedly, the knife was raised high, poised to strike. He launched himself at Sabatino's knife hand, dimly hearing Gabrielle's shout. The next thing he knew, he hit the floor rolling, tangled up in a mess of dog and woman.

"What the hell did you do that for?" Devlin asked her, shoving himself out from under them. "The bastard pulled a knife on you!"

Her attention was divided between wrestling the thrashing dog and the man who was now putting away his knife as though nothing had ever happened. "He pulled a knife on Rocky," she said, panting from effort. "And you'd have gotten killed if you'd reached him."

"Purely by accident," Sabatino added, his dark eyes glimmering, looking pleased at the thought. "I was merely protecting myself. Gabriela, put the animal out now."

Gabrielle and Devlin rose together, her hand still wrapped in the dog's collar. "Do it," Devlin said to her, not taking his eyes off Sabatino.

"While Sabatino and I have a discussion about the proper time and place to see your lawyer."

She started to argue but Rocky began barking and growling again. Devlin looked at Gabrielle and saw her flash a warning glare at Sabatino before she dragged the dog away.

"The knife," Devlin said. "Take it out real slow and drop it."

The bastard laughed. "Why? Are you going to make me, pretty boy?"

His hand twitched with the need to slam his fist into that sneering face but he controlled it, knowing the man's game. "It's a simple matter to call the cops and tell them you held your lawyer at knifepoint, Sabatino."

The other man shrugged. "Very well. If you insist." With exaggerated care, he reached in and slowly withdrew the knife, then flung it down with a practiced twist of his wrist. The tip of the blade stuck in the wood floor, quivering an inch in front of Devlin's bare foot.

"Devlin." Gabrielle's voice sliced through the tension vibrating like the knife blade stuck in the floor between the two men. They both looked at her. "This is my house. I'd appreciate you letting me handle this."

Let her handle it? Sure he would—right after he ground the sucker's smile into his face and then ripped him apart limb by limb. He still hadn't recovered from thinking Sabatino intended the knife for Gabrielle.

She either read his mind or the expression on his face, because she stepped between them before he could do anything. "What do you want?" she asked Sabatino.

"A moment with you alone."

"No," Devlin said, his jaw clenched. "No way in hell."

Smiling derisively, Sabatino spoke to Gabrielle. "Quite the jealous lover, isn't he? Understandable, though, with a woman of your . . ." He looked her over leisurely, obviously taking note of her tousled hair, her robe, her bare feet, and finished, "Your many charms, *signorina. Tanta magnifica*—"

Devlin had started forward, intending to rip Sabatino's slimy tongue out of his mouth, but Gabrielle slapped her hand on his arm and gripped it tightly, restraining him as she interrupted Sabatino herself.

"Say what you want and then get out," she said flatly. "And don't contact me at home about your case."

"Ah, but you see, *cara*," he said silkily, "I didn't come about my case."

"Cut to the chase, Sabatino," Devlin said, his temper spiking into the stratosphere. "Why are you here?"

"For the usual reasons one goes to see a beautiful woman," he answered Devlin. Their gazes held for a tight moment, then Sabatino turned to Gabrielle. "I wasn't aware that you were"—he spread his hands, gesturing at Devlin—"involved with someone."

"Now you know," Devlin said, wondering how long he would last before he went for Sabatino's throat. "So you can leave."

"My apologies for the . . . intrusion." Sabatino inclined his head and bent to pick up his knife.

"Leave it."

"And if I don't?" he asked, one eyebrow lifting arrogantly.

"Don't forget I'm a lawyer, Sabatino. I can get as down and dirty as I need to."

To Devlin's surprise, Sabatino left the knife without further argument. At the door he gazed at Gabrielle for a long moment. "Always the pretty boy, isn't it, Gabriela? I would have thought after—"

She interrupted him with a few words, spoken softly in Italian. Devlin had no idea what she said, but obviously Sabatino did. His mouth snapped shut, and he and Gabrielle stared at each other while silence ticked by with the sort of tension that pervaded a courtroom before a murder verdict is read. Without another word, Sabatino turned his back and left.

Gabrielle shut the door, leaning her head against it for a moment. Straightening, she squared her shoulders and turned to look at him, her face wiped clean of emotion.

Oh, no, sweetheart, he thought. That won't work this time. This time, he intended to get answers. "What in the bloody hell is going on be-tween you and Sabatino, Gabrielle?"

She stared at him, just stood there staring at him in the taut silence. "Nothing," she said, fi-nally. "Nothing's going on."

"That won't fly, sweetheart." Devlin grasped her arm with one hand, cupping her chin with his other to force her to look at him. "Tell me."

No longer expressionless, a series of emotions crossed her face. Anger, confusion, fear. It was the latter that shadowed her eyes as well, Devlin thought, darkening them to a deep jade. Beneath it all, he sensed a torment he didn't understand.

"He—this isn't the first time he's been here."

"Go on," Devlin said harshly, dropping his hand to her arm, but still holding her gaze.

She drew herself up, seeming to get hold of herself. "He came over a few days ago. With the same agenda. I told him to forget it, but obviously, he doesn't listen well."

His fingers tightened on her arms as he stared at her, trying to hear what she wasn't saying. "Did he touch you?"

"Devlin—"

"I asked if he touched you."

"No." She swore at him and jerked out of his grasp. "No, he didn't. Don't go all Neanderthal about this. He hasn't done anything a lot of men haven't tried. It's not a crime to ask a woman out."

Devlin muttered an obscenity, knowing what she said was reasonable, but he didn't feel reasonable about Sabatino. He paced away a step and turned back to her. "Sabatino is your client. What's he doing hitting on you?"

She looked at him like he was nuts, then she laughed in disbelief. "Oh, come on, Devlin. You can't tell me none of your clients has ever hit on you."

His smile was bitter. No, he couldn't say that. Celine had considered sleeping with him a small price to pay for his getting her off that murder charge. Too bad he'd been too stupid to realize her game. Or her guilt. "Remind me to tell you a story sometime. But right now, we're talking about you and Sabatino. You can't deny there's something between the two of you."

Cocking her head, she narrowed her eyes and cast a speculative look at him. "You almost sound like you're jealous. Is that what this is about?"

Damn, she knew all the moves. Why should he be surprised? "Good try, but it's not working. I've seen you shiver when you get near him, Gabrielle." Devlin stepped closer, his gaze boring into hers. "I think you hate Sabatino. I think he makes your skin crawl. Now tell me, why do you hate a man you just met a few weeks ago?"

"You're overreacting. I don't like him, I'll admit that, but you're imagining things."

"Overreacting?" He bracketed her chin with his hand and stared at her. Her pulse beat at her throat, steady, not jumpy. "Maybe, but I don't think so." Then he swore and pulled her into his arms. "I thought the knife was for you." A bloody, sickening image flashed through his mind of that gleaming blade and what it might have done to Gabrielle's delicate flesh.

She hugged him tightly and buried her face against his shoulder. "No, when he came over before, he—he said he hated dogs." Her voice was low, hesitant. "I had a dog once. Someone killed him. Cut his throat." Devlin felt her swallow convulsively before she continued, "So when I saw the knife, I knew it was for Rocky."

"I don't like the way he looks at you," he muttered, his lips against her hair. "Or the way he talks to you. I don't like all those Italian endearments he's always saying to you. The next time I hear him say *bellisima*, I'm going to break his face."

Gabrielle gave a muffled laugh. "It just means pretty. It's not an obscenity."

"It is the way he says it." They were silent, holding each other, absorbed in each other as much of the strain faded. After a time, Devlin loosened his hold and dropped a kiss on her lips before leading her to the couch.

"What did you say to him?" he asked her, wrapping his arm around her shoulders. Her brow furrowed; she looked confused. "When you spoke to him in Italian," he added, "just before he left."

For a moment she looked blank, but then she smiled. "I'm not sure of the exact translation, but it's an extremely idiomatic way of saying get lost."

"You're fluent in Italian?" There was nothing in that. Why did it make him uneasy?

"Not fluent. I know some phrases. A high school boyfriend taught me a chosen few."

His heart twisted. Literally twisted in his chest. She was lying. It sounded plausible, but she was lying. Devlin didn't know how he knew it, but he did. Why would she lie about speaking Italian? And what else was she lying about? He wanted her to trust him. He wanted to trust her.

But he didn't.

The worst thing was, it didn't matter. Not one damned bit. He was still in love with her.

TWELVE

Gabrielle took a sip of coffee and sighed, wondering how police station coffee could taste two days old at eight o'clock on a Monday morning. Didn't they ever make it fresh? "Here," she said to Devlin, thumbing through the stack of police reports and slapping a pile down in front of him. "These are some of the ones I was reading when I started feeling ill." She'd made sure to give him the file that held the police error. It would be better, she decided, if Devlin found it himself, and she had no doubt he would.

He sipped his own coffee, made a face, and started looking through them, while Gabrielle pretended to do the same with her own stack. She flipped the pages now and again, but her mind was on other things. Such as the previous day's near disaster with Franco. If she could only tell Devlin the truth . . .

But how?

She looked over at him, and her heart swelled with love. It was crazy that she could be so in love with him after such a short time. And even more unbelievable that he had fallen for her too. They'd only known each other a matter of weeks. Though she had to admit he was gorgeous, and her attraction had begun with that, she hadn't fallen for Devlin because of his looks.

The day Marcie Field came into his office, she'd realized she was in serious trouble. Not because he'd helped Marcie, though that had surprised and touched her. No, it was when he'd tried to give Marcie some money on the sly and she had thrown her arms around his neck and cried. The expression on Devlin's face had been priceless. And Gabrielle had fallen in love with him.

If she told him of her past, what would he do, what would he think? That she was a liar, certainly. God only knew what he'd think about the fact that she'd kept so much from him. Pertinent information that he had a right to know as her partner on the case. Would he think she'd withheld the truth to further her career at the expense of his? And how could she deny her actions had been intended to save her career?

The thought of telling Devlin the whole sordid story about Franco and Vito was too much right now. She'd lose him. The first man she'd loved since that long-ago day when Franco told her that her father had bought off her fiancé for ten thousand dollars. No, it didn't bear thinking of.

Devlin caught her staring at him and gave her one of his knee-weakening smiles before returning to the reports. Those smiles of his were lethal, she thought, remembering the previous afternoon. They'd gone to his place, an apartment in a beautiful Highland Park high-rise, so that he could change clothes. The elevator ride had been memorable. They'd barely made it out of the elevator and into his apartment before making love again. The man was definitely dangerous. She had no business thinking of lovemaking when disaster stalked her every move.

"If you don't stop looking at me that way," Devlin murmured, "we're not going to get very far with these reports."

She managed to toss him a saucy smile. "Hold that thought." Looking him over, she added, "Until after work."

"I'll do my best," he said, and winked.

A few minutes later he spoke again. "I found something."

"What?" Nerves had her knocking over her cup of coffee. Gabrielle swore as she and Devlin grabbed up papers, barely avoiding the river of brown liquid seeping across the table and dribbling onto the floor.

"Are you okay?" he asked, giving her a keen glance.

"Fine. Just clumsy," she said, willing her hands to stop shaking. "What did you find?"

He gazed at her for a few seconds longer, then looked at the paper in his hand. "This one. Looks like a break in the chain of custody of the evidence."

"Let me see," she said, holding out her hand. He gave it to her, and she ran her gaze over it, pretending to read. She felt like slime, like gutter refuse, lying to him like she was. But the alternative to lying was . . . impossible. She raised her eyes to meet his. "They never signed the evidence in at the evidence room of the station."

"Nope." His eyes gleamed bright with the rush of discovery. Gabrielle recognized the look, knowing she'd worn it herself many times. Devlin was gearing up to spring the trap on the DA's case.

Leaning over her to point to the paragraph in question, he continued, "Everything's tidy until the transportation officer left the seized evidence at the evidence room. The officer in charge of the room never signed the form testifying to what time it passed into his hands."

"Which means . . ." Her voice trailed off.

"This"—he waved the report—"means we can get Sabatino off. Request a hearing with the judge and the DA, ask the judge to allow the case to be dropped. The evidence in question is the prosecution's primary case against him. They don't have jack to support the charges without that evidence. We may not even go to trial."

Not go to trial, she thought. Get Franco off and not have to go to court over it. Surely Franco would leave her alone then, once he was free of the charges against him. He'd slink back to New York, if she was lucky, and she'd never have to see him again. And she could forget about her past as if it had never happened.

Devlin would never have to know a thing.

If she told herself that enough times, maybe she could even begin to believe it.

Late that night Devlin tracked Gabrielle to her office, reminding him of another night he'd found her working after hours. But tonight he wouldn't go home alone and frustrated. Not sexually frustrated anyway, though the nagging certainty that she was lying to him was wearing him down.

He knocked and shoved open her office door, expecting to find her buried in papers, but she was sitting with her chair turned toward the darkened window and apparently hadn't heard him come in. Brooding over missing that police error?

In her place, he'd be mad as hell at himself, but maybe Gabrielle had managed to blow it off as simply the effect of illness. Still, it had to rankle an attorney with her reputation to miss something a second-year law student could have picked up.

And Devlin had found the weak link within ten minutes of looking at those reports. Being lovers didn't mean they weren't still rivals at CG&S.

How was that going to affect their future relationship? He knew they would have to deal with the issue, but since he didn't know any answers he wasn't particularly eager to pursue the topic right now.

"The hearing is set for day after tomorrow," he said, and closed the door behind him.

At his words, she spun the chair around and looked at him. "Day after tomorrow? That's quick."

He shrugged and walked over to her, propping a hip on her desk. "Judge Gray had an opening. I've told Sabatino."

"You saw him?"

"No," he said, and laughed shortly. "Called him. I was afraid I'd punch his face in if I saw him in person."

"Don't do it," she said, fear flashing in her eyes. "Promise me you won't."

Curious, he leaned over and traced his forefinger down her cheek. "Why does he frighten you so much, Gabrielle?"

She grabbed hold of his hand. "Devlin, he's Mafia. That's enough to frighten anyone. I don't want you getting hurt."

"As long as he leaves you alone, there's nothing to worry about," he said, squeezing her hand and releasing it.

"I can deal with him." She angled her chin up.

"Yeah. So can I." His hand curled into a fist as he thought about the satisfaction he'd get wiping some of those pretty Italian words off Sabatino's mouth.

"Devlin," Gabrielle said sharply. "Promise me you won't fight with him."

Rather than lie, he ignored that. "You know"—he pushed himself away from the desk and paced across the floor with a restless energy—"this is the first time in a long time that I wouldn't have minded losing a case. If it meant Sabatino would have gotten what's coming to him . . ." Regretfully, he shook his head. "Now the feds have no way of getting him to talk. Not that he would have, anyway. Only a fool would face Donati after ratting on him. Whatever else he is, Sabatino is no fool."

"There are lots of other known criminals that Sabatino's had dealings with. Donati isn't the only one the feds want him to talk about."

"No, but he's one of the big ones, even if he has toned his operation down in recent years. And from what I've heard, Sabatino's the closest thing Donati has to a son." Snatching at a memory, he frowned, but he couldn't quite grab it. "There was some story—"

"You'd never throw a case," she said, interrupting him.

Surprised by the abrupt statement, he stopped pacing to stare at her. "No, I wouldn't. But that's not to say there haven't been cases I wished I hadn't won." He thought of Celine, his mouth twisting in a bitter smile. "And cases I should never have taken in the first place."

Gabrielle gazed at him for a moment, then leaned back in her chair and crossed her legs. "Who was she?"

"How do you know it was a woman?"

"An educated guess," she said, smiling wryly. "Want to talk about it?"

Did he? He wasn't sure. He stalked to the window, leaning an arm against the frame as he gazed out at the night. "Her name was Celine. Charged with murder one in the death of her husband. It happened during my public defender days." Silent for a moment, he let the memories seep back. "God, I still can't believe how dumb I was," he muttered. "I got her off scot-free. Not even a manslaughter charge. The DA screwed up his case against her or he'd have had her cold. It was quite a coup for me, even considering the prosecution's screwup."

"Was she guilty?"

Devlin shot her a grim smile over his shoulder. "As sin. And I was the sucker who believed she was innocent." Gabrielle winced, and he turned back to the window. "Yeah. It's not much fun to be made a complete fool of. She took off with her lover the day after the verdict came down."

He heard her chair squeak as she pushed it back, then her hand fell on his shoulder and squeezed. Warm sympathy flowed from her as she pressed herself against his back and slid her arms around his waist. It felt strange, telling her something he'd never told anyone. Now, if only she would come clean with him . . .

"You weren't a fool," she said quietly. "We all get sucked in sometimes."

"Celine was good, I'll admit that. A great actress, in bed, in court. Hell, she was great wherever she needed to be." And she'd reeled him in like the dumbest bass in the lake.

"Don't," Gabrielle whispered, tightening her arms, pressing her cheek against the back of his shoulder. "It doesn't matter now."

"Doesn't it?" He turned and gripped her upper arms, staring into her eyes. "I swore after Celine I'd never let another woman get to me."

Gabrielle said nothing, but her lips trembled as though in invitation. Her mouth looked rose-petal soft, enough to tempt a saint to sin. He knew what fantastically wicked things she could do with that mouth, and it fueled his anger that he could want her so much and trust her so little.

Releasing her arms, he slid his hands to the small of her back and pulled her tightly against him. Her eyes widened, the pupils dilating as her breath started coming faster, her pulse fluttering in her throat like a wild thing. He wanted to kiss her there. Put his mouth against her throat and drink in her heartbeat, steep himself in the dizzying, sensual taste of her skin. To take her, there in her office where she looked so proper and in control. Wanted to watch the transformation, see her shatter when he pushed her to the edge and over it. Wanted her not to matter so much, and damned both of them because she did.

"And I never have let a woman get to me again. Until you," he said, and crushed her mouth beneath his. Her lips opened, and he invaded, tasting the hot, sweet temptation she offered. She moaned and wrapped her arms around his neck, holding him as tightly as he held her. He left her mouth, bending her back over his arm to kiss her neck, to savor the pulse beating at its hollow.

Shoving papers aside, he laid her back on the bare strip of dark wood and opened her blouse with two quick jerks of his hands. Through her lacy bra, he caressed her breasts, smiling as he brought her nipples to stiff peaks against his palms, then rolled them with his fingers. "You've never said"—he leaned down and covered one of her nipples with his mouth, drew it in and sucked on it slowly, flicked his tongue against it before releasing it—"what this means to you."

Her answer was an incoherent moan and her chest lifting to offer him more.

He took more, sliding his hands up under her skirt, past the sheer stockings to the garter belt he knew she wore. One of those creations men dreamed about but few women wore. "Is this just great sex . . . ?" One by one, he popped her garters, then tugged her panties down and glided them off her legs. "Or is there something more? Tell me, Gabrielle."

"More," she said.

He smiled down at her. "I think that's a double entendre."

"Don't . . . tease." Her back arched as his fingers slipped inside her, withdrew, slid in again. "The door . . ." she said, gasping for breath. "Lock the . . . lock the door."

He kissed her mouth. Long, deep, hot. "You haven't answered my question."

She pushed up to sit on the edge of the desk, with his hands still beneath her skirt, taunting her. Her hair had loosened, tumbled over her shoulders; her eyes were heavy-lidded, dark green and beautiful. Her mouth was full, lush, inviting him to partake of the pleasure, and he wanted to immerse himself in her and never come out. She reached for his slacks, unbuttoned and unzipped them.

"I think you're an incredibly sexy jerk"—her hand curled around his aching flesh, and she stroked slowly up and down the length of him— "who I'm in love with. Now will you lock the damn door and finish making love to me?"

Devlin decided he might have outsmarted himself, because at that moment he didn't think he could leave her long enough to get to the door. She took her hands out of his pants and gave him a seductive smile. "Hurry up," she whispered, her voice husky with promise, and blew him a kiss.

He made it to the door and back within seconds. An instant after that, he buried himself to the hilt inside her. She was soft and wet, and she tightened around him like an erotic dream. No matter how much he wanted to, he was too far gone to make it last. He stroked into her once, then twice before exploding deep inside her. A step behind him, she cried out as she peaked.

The last tremors faded, and he heard her whisper, "I love you, Devlin."

Even as he smiled, he wondered why he'd never heard a sadder sound than the sigh she gave afterward.

THIRTEEN

Wednesday morning dawned, as inevitable as death and taxes. Gabrielle felt like she was going to her own trial rather than her client's hearing for dismissal of his case. She hadn't been able to resist being with Devlin the night before, but he'd left her place very early that morning to get ready for court. Hopefully she could avoid him until they met in the courtroom. Otherwise he'd be bound to wonder how she'd ever gotten a reputation as a competent attorney, let alone lived up to her nickname. Jumpy, spacey, nervous as a cat on a live electric wire didn't begin to describe her, and she had the gut-wrenching certainty she'd have another panic attack the moment she stepped inside the courthouse.

She stared at the long expanse of concrete steps stretching before her. One foot in front of the other, she climbed slowly to the courthouse doors, each successive step becoming harder to take. Her fingertips began to tingle. A tendril of tension crawled up her spine, a warning signal of more to come.

"Hi, beautiful," she heard Devlin say from behind her.

The panicked feeling faded as she turned to smile and wait for him, remembering the first time he'd said that to her. Though he didn't kiss her, his roguish smile and the expression in his eyes told her what he was thinking. She was thinking about it too.

"Seen Sabatino anywhere?" he asked, glancing around as he caught up to her. "He said he'd meet us here a little early."

"Not a sign of him." Thank God for small blessings. She didn't want to be around Franco one more second than absolutely necessary. Checking her watch, she started up the stairs again. "We've still got half an hour, though."

"Are you sure you want me to present the motion for dismissal?"

Surprised, she looked at him as he held the heavy door for her. "We agreed on that last night."

"Yes, I know. But I—" He dragged her to one side of the hallway and said, "What's going on with you? You didn't even make a token protest to my presenting the motion. In fact, you insisted I do it. Is it because you missed the report? Is that what this is about?"

"Devlin, we hashed this out last night. It's a

minor point. What difference does it make who presents it?"

"Theoretically, none. But you and I both know that Sid's watching this case with extra attention."

Sid. The partnership. In the wake of everything else, she'd all but forgotten that aspect of the case. "Just do it, Devlin." He searched her face, seemed about to speak, then shrugged and continued down the hall.

Walking beside him, Gabrielle felt more like herself, more in control than she had in a long time. Maybe because her crisis was finally going to end, one way or the other. And she took heart from the fact that she'd beaten back the panic attack that had started outside the courthouse.

As they neared the courtroom she saw him. Franco Sabatino stood motionless at the end of the hallway, watching them. Dark, so dark, she thought. Black suit, black hair, black soul. Waiting for her, her own particular hell on earth. She looked into the dark eyes of his soul and knew she'd never be free of him.

Her heart started to pound. The tingling began again at the base of her neck, spreading tentacles from the top of her head all the way to her toes. Furiously, she fought it back, but it advanced, insidious, persistent, nibbling at the edges of her mind. She broke into a light sweat, and her heart slammed against her chest.

"Gabrielle, what's—Oh, crap," she heard Devlin say, as though from a long distance.

Mumbling an excuse, she bolted for the ladies' room, thanking God it was just down the hall. Devlin would know, of course, what had happened. Now that he'd actually witnessed her having one attack, there was no way he wouldn't recognize the warning signs of another.

Hiding in a stall, fumbling with her paper bag, the routine came back to her quickly because of the recent attacks. Just as though she'd never had a break of several years. Funny how quickly she'd become reaccustomed to them. Closing her eyes, she bent her head and breathed into the bag.

Eventually, she dragged herself to the sink and splashed water on her face. Taking a paper towel to wipe away the excess moisture, she caught a glimpse of herself in the mirror and stared. *This* was Gabrielle Rousseau, Queen of Sharks? This pitiful excuse for a woman? With her haunted eyes, her shoulders slumped in defeat, her resigned, hopeless expression, she bore more resemblance to a minnow than to any self-respecting shark.

No, by God, she thought. *I'm not going to let fear rule me. I won't be Franco's victim any longer.*

When she emerged a few minutes later, Devlin was waiting for her. He took her arm, and his grip wasn't gentle. "Are you all right?"

"Fine." She met his gaze defiantly, daring him to argue.

He didn't argue, but kept hold of her arm as he led her toward Franco. "We'll talk about this later," he said, and his tone brooked no argument.

"Ah, my esteemed attorneys," Franco said when they reached him. "It seems I owe you my thanks."

"Save it for later," Devlin said. "Let's go." He held the courtroom door open, waiting for Gabrielle to pass through it.

Squaring her shoulders, she stepped inside the courtroom. Her nerve endings sizzled, this time with the familiar rush of excitement that facing a legal battle always brought with it. They took their seats, and she spoke to Devlin.

"I've changed my mind. I'd like to present the motion for dismissal." It wasn't fair of her to ask him, considering he had almost as much to gain from presenting the case as she did. And considering that she knew if she asked, he wouldn't deny her. Yet, unfair or not, she did ask him. If she didn't face the fear now and conquer it, she would never believe in herself again.

He studied her for a long moment, then nodded. "It's yours," he said.

The case went like a dream. Gabrielle presented the motion for dismissal, with the police report entered as proof regarding a break in the chain of custody of the evidence. The signature of the evidence room officer was clearly missing, and Gabrielle was able to cast considerable doubt that the prosecution's primary evidence had been properly safeguarded.

The DA fought the motion, maintaining that since the evidence resided in the police station, the lack of signature was a mere technicality, but he knew as well as Gabrielle that that particular evidence was now worthless. He was also unable to present any further evidence to prove the defendant's guilt.

While clearly displeased to free a known Mafia gangster, the judge agreed with the defense's logic. Half an hour after he entered the courtroom, the judge dismissed the case of the *United States* v. *Franco Sabatino*. Franco Sabatino was cleared of all charges.

"Congratulations," Devlin said to Gabrielle as they gathered their papers. "You were impressive."

Oddly enough, Gabrielle felt a quiver of pleasure at the victory. "Thanks."

"My deepest appreciation," Franco said, offering Devlin his hand. Devlin took it, though Gabrielle had the feeling he'd rather have punched him.

Franco turned to her. "And to you, *mi bellisima avvocatessa*, my eternal gratitude." Before she could stop him, he'd carried her hand to his lips. "And devotion," he murmured, turning her hand over and pressing a kiss into her palm.

Gabrielle jerked out of his grasp, glancing at Devlin for fear of his reaction. His eyes had narrowed, and she saw his hands curl into fists. She grabbed his arm and in its tautness felt his anger about to explode. "Don't. Come on, let's get out of here."

She didn't *think* Devlin would punch out his client in a court of law, but she couldn't be positive. After a tense moment, the three of them left the room.

No one said a word as they walked down the hallway. Then a woman called out Devlin's name. Gabrielle saw Marcie Field waving at him.

"Damn," he muttered. "I've got to go see her a minute. Wait for me. I won't be long." He gave Franco a warning glare and stalked off.

"Convenient," Franco said, watching him go. "I find him very much in the way."

"You and I have nothing further to discuss," Gabrielle said, confronting him. "I took your case, we got you off, and now you can go. And leave me the hell alone."

"Ah, but Gabriela," he said, his smile patronizing, "that's where you're wrong."

"Let's get this over with." She crossed her arms over her chest. "What is it you want?"

"You, of course. Come back with me. Marry me and come home. Reconcile with your father."

Her mouth dropped open as she stared. "You're insane."

"If insane means being in love—"

"Love?" Thinking of Franco and love in the same sentence nauseated her. "This isn't about love . . ." Her voice trailed off as she thought over his words. Reconcile with her father, he'd said. Of course. *Vito* was the key. "What have you done? You've fallen out of his favor, haven't you? Has Vito finally figured out what you're really like?"

Franco's expression darkened, and for a moment he lost the suave mask he wore. But only for a moment. "Come home with me, Gabriela. I want you. Vito wants you. You have no choice, not really."

"Why is this so important to you? Tell me why you want me. The truth, not this drivel of love."

His eyes narrowed, and he almost snarled at her. "You were always too smart for a woman. It would have been better to keep your illusions. Vito is—" He hesitated, and irritation washed over his face. "Shall we say Vito is displeased with me? If I can bring you back to him, and as my wife . . ." Franco raised his shoulders and spread his hands. "Why then he'll have to name me as heir. The Donati empire isn't what it once was, but when I am in control it will be powerful again."

So simple. She should have recognized his motives immediately. "Your machinations are of no interest to me, Franco. That life hasn't been mine for fourteen years. How can you think I'd even consider going back with you?"

He glanced toward Devlin, who was still talking to Marcie Field. Then he faced her and smiled. She'd never seen a smile personify evil until she saw Franco's face at that moment.

"It would give me great pleasure," he said, his voice deep and silky smooth, "to kill your lover myself. To gut him like the cur he is. Remember what happened when you defied me before?"

Suddenly she was there again, in her darkened

bedroom shouting curses at Franco, refusing to marry him. And then the fight, the desperate struggle against hands that ripped her clothes and rained blows on her face and body. Her dog Samson barking madly, hurling himself at the intruder, trying to defend her. In her mind's eye she saw Franco's exhilaration, the near sexual thrill he gained as he slit Samson's throat and watched the blood drain from the dog's body. And the stamp of arousal on his face as he came for her, blood dripping from the knife in his hand.

She turned away, toward Devlin, and memories of him flicked through her mind. How he looked in the courtroom or when arguing a point with her. His expression when Marcie Field had thrown her arms around him. The way he'd looked the first time he told her he loved her. Images of him comforting her in the police station stairwell. The two of them making love. Devlin smiling, laughing, teasing, comforting, loving. Loving. She wrapped her arms around her stomach and willed herself to breathe.

"Yes, I see you do remember," Franco said, his voice replete with malice. "I would enjoy that very much, Gabriela. The choice is yours."

He left her there, with her heart beating a slow drumroll of despair and Devlin walking toward her.

The next few hours passed in a blur for Gabrielle. She met briefly with Sid, setting up a meeting for the next day, checked over her caseload for the next few weeks, and talked to Devlin as if she had never heard Franco threaten to kill him. Inside she cursed herself for her stupidity, her weakness. Because of her criminal negligence in ignoring what she knew about Franco, she'd put Devlin at risk.

How could she stop Franco? Before, her only solution had been to flee. But running would solve nothing now. And it would leave Devlin in danger. Only one person had the power to stop Franco.

Vito Donati.

And only one person had the power to convince Vito to do it. Gabriela Donati, Vito's daughter.

Gabrielle left the office early and went home, still with no idea of what she would say when she talked to her father. She didn't plan a speech; she decided to simply ask him for help, as she had one other time. Memories washed over her again, and she heard the voices. Hers, Franco's, and Vito's.

"Gabriela, you're being absurd," Franco had said. "It's what your father wants. What I want. Marry me and forget Ben. He left you easily enough."

Ignoring him, she had turned to her father. "I'll never forgive you. Never. And I'll never marry Franco. The only thing you can do for me is let me go. Give me a new identity and let me walk out. I don't ever want to see you again."

He hadn't believed her. Hadn't imagined that

she would view his act of paying off the man she loved as the betrayal it was. Hadn't believed that her refusal to marry Franco was anything more than a willful child's defiance.

It had taken her near-death in the fall from her bedroom window the night Franco came to her to convince her father she meant what she said. Vito had thought her dive out the window a suicide attempt, rather than what it was—her only means of escaping Franco. Gabrielle hadn't considered the danger when she'd taken the only way out of her bedroom, and to this day she couldn't remember exactly how she'd come to fall. Since Franco's face was the last thing she remembered, she suspected he had played a large part in it. She had never corrected her father's mistaken conclusion, because she'd known what Vito would do had he known the truth. Had he known what Franco had tried to do to her, he would have killed him.

In the end, Vito let her go.

Gabrielle picked up the phone and dialed, wondering what she would do if the number was no longer in service. If it were only herself, she would take the consequences, but she couldn't allow anything to happen to Devlin, and she knew of no other way to protect him.

"*Sì.*"

Fourteen years since she'd heard his voice. She closed her eyes and swallowed hard before she spoke. "*Papà*, it's me, Gabriela."

There was a silence so intense, she thought she

might break. But it was the voice on the other end of the line that broke. "Gabriela? *E tu? Vero?*"

"Yes." Tears stung her eyes, and she blinked them away. "*Sì, Papà.*"

"Are you coming home?"

The hope in his voice choked her with emotion. "I can't." Her fingers tightened on the receiver. "You know I can't."

"I've missed you, Gabriela. Every day of my life. Are you happy?"

She thought of Devlin and what might have been. Devlin and what could never be, not after she told him the truth. "I'm in trouble and I need your help."

"You have only to ask. You know that."

"It's Franco. There's a man I—Franco has threatened to kill someone I know. I want you to stop him."

Vito cursed. "It will be taken care of. I warned him to stay away from you."

"I wondered—at first I thought you had sent him."

"No, Gabriela, I swore to you I would not. Have I not kept my word?"

"Yes." Her throat was clogged with sorrow and useless tears. It took a moment before she could speak again. "Don't kill him. Promise you won't kill him. Just make him leave, and make sure he doesn't hurt . . . anyone."

"Why do you care if he dies, Gabriela?"

"I don't want his blood on my hands." And that was why she hadn't told her father the truth about that night fourteen years before. She wanted no murders staining her soul.

"This man Franco has threatened. Do you love him?"

"Yes."

"Will you marry him?"

"No." Her eyes closed, and opened. "It isn't going to work out like that."

"Are you certain?"

Dead sure. "Yes."

"I'm sorry for your pain. There's nothing I can do for you about that, but I'll take care of Franco. Remember I love you."

"Thank you." Hot tears slid down her cheeks. "I love you too, *Papà*." She cradled the receiver, buried her head in her hands, and wept for the father she'd loved. The father she still loved.

Eventually, her tears slowed. Gabrielle knew she'd made the only possible decision she could make. She couldn't live the life Vito had chosen; she had to live her own. Any contact, given those circumstances, was dangerous to them both. If she couldn't live in his world, she couldn't risk any association with it. And the path she'd chosen had been the right one for her. She knew that, was at peace with that. If only her path could have included her father. But it never could.

And now the truth faced her with another pain.

She wiped the last tears away, drew in a shuddering breath, and resolved to face her present. She would find a way to tell Devlin she was Gabriela Donati, daughter of Vito Donati, once the most powerful Mafia don in the country.

FOURTEEN

Gabrielle's fingers stilled on the keyboard, the haunting melody fading slowly away. The music hadn't soothed her, but she knew of nothing that would. It was hard to find anything soothing when facing the ruins of your career . . . and your heart.

"Shouldn't that be a song of victory?" Devlin asked from the front doorway. "We won the case. Why the melancholia?" He stood on the threshold, his suit coat slung over his shoulder, blond hair glinting in the moonlight spilling in from behind him.

She hadn't heard him open the door, but caught up as she'd been in the music, in memories and dreams, that was no surprise. "But what price victory?" she murmured.

He came into the room, throwing his coat over a chair and pitching his tie after it. "I don't know," he said, watching her. "That's one of the things we need to talk about."

She stayed at the piano, trying to drum up her nerve and talk to him. The sooner she did it . . . The sooner she told him, the sooner she would lose him. She would never again see him smile at her or hear his laugh. Never again hear his words of love or see love fill his eyes as he looked at her. Never feel the touch of his lips, of his hands, the weight of his body upon hers. Never touch him, never feel his passion, never make love with him again.

Her chest hurt. Tears stung her eyes, and her throat closed up. How useless to cry, she thought, when her world was about to fall apart. But she could think of no way to stop it, no way to fix it.

Devlin crossed the room to her, sat beside her on the piano bench, and studied her face. Leaning over, he kissed her mouth briefly, drawing away even as her lips clung to his. She wondered if he felt the desperation in her kiss.

"You look like hell," he said, laying his palm against her cheek. "Want to tell me why?"

"No," she whispered truthfully. She slid her arms around his waist, ran her hands up his back, and kissed him again, ignoring the voice chanting "the last time" in her mind.

"But you're going to tell me," he murmured. His hands on her arms, he pushed her away from him to look at her.

His eyes were dark gray and compassionate. As

if she could tell him anything, and he would understand. But would he? How would he look at her when he knew? With hate? Disgust? Could he forgive her? No, she knew the answer to that.

Didn't they deserve one last time? One more time before the truth wrecked everything they might have had? Was it so wrong of her to want that? So wrong to take it?

"Before we talk—" Her voice stuttered, stumbled. Drawing in a deep breath, she started again. "There's something I want, before we talk."

"What?" He asked the question softly, still gazing into her eyes.

"Tonight. I want tonight with you."

He frowned. "Meaning what?"

"No past." Leaning into him, she kissed his mouth. "No future," she whispered, leaving his mouth to trace kisses along his jaw. "Only the present. Right now, right here."

His expression hardened, his tone grew harsher as he drew away from her again. "I didn't come here for sex, Gabrielle. I came to hear the truth. The truth about you and Franco Sabatino."

"And I'll tell you. But not . . . not tonight. Please, Devlin, can't we have this last night?" Their gazes met, held. "You," she said huskily. "Me. One last night." If she had to live in hell for the rest of her life, she wanted a slice of heaven to take with her. Was one final night, a final good-bye too much to ask for?

One last night, Devlin thought, staring at her.

Was the truth so bad? Gabrielle obviously thought so. Would it hurt to give her, and himself, this night? More important, could he refuse her?

His silence became his assent. Her mouth traced a moist, fiery path down his neck to his chest as her fingers unbuttoned his shirt. Her tongue flicked over one of his nipples, then the other, gently rasping, her teeth nipping until he groaned with pleasure. Her hands glided over his skin, learning him, caressing him, sending tremors of excitement rippling through his body. If he was going to stop her, it had to be soon.

He didn't stop her. Instead, he sank his hands into her thick brown hair, so soft and rich, it flowed over his hands and forearms like strands of dark silk. His fingers pressed against her head as she moved lower, her tongue whirling in patterns across his chest, his abdomen, flicking into his navel as her hands tugged at his belt. In moments, she had the buckle unfastened and his zipper down. When she took him in her hands his mind clouded, an instant away from shutting down entirely. "Gabrielle—" He started to speak, but couldn't. He could only suck in his breath, barely able to breathe.

"Don't talk," she said, her hands and her mouth on him, hot, vibrant, tempting. "Just . . . let me. Let me love you."

He sensed it was a mistake, but he didn't stop her. He gave himself up to the warm, sensual magic of her mouth, the erotic sensations that exploded along his skin at her touch. Desire surged hard, pumping through his bloodstream with a furious rhythm.

She knelt in front of him, her mouth leading him into realms he'd never visited before, even though he'd thought himself an experienced man. But there had never been Gabrielle before. Seductive, exciting as it was, he didn't want to go alone. "Come here," he said hoarsely, pulling her up so he could kiss her mouth. She allowed him the kiss, but when he would have continued, she shook her head.

"Let me," she whispered.

"I want you with me."

"Devlin, let me," she said again.

Her eyes were a dark jade green and haunted with something he couldn't name. He gazed at her for a long moment, then put his hands in her hair and watched her neck bend, her head slowly drop.

Later, he led her to the bedroom, and they made love again. And he knew, with each gentle stroke, each lingering caress, each deep, searching kiss, that this was good-bye.

Devlin woke in the early hours of dawn and listened to Gabrielle's even breathing, felt the warmth of her naked body curving into his. Her scent stroked his nostrils, imprinting itself in his memory; her skin felt smooth and tempting against his. He glanced down at her and smiled, thinking he'd never known a woman who remained in his mind like she did. A woman who could distract him with a simple smile or a touch.

Or something not so simple, he thought, his smile fading. Like the night before, when he had wanted answers and she had asked for one last night.

And Monday night at her office, he remembered, when they'd been talking about Sabatino's case. Sabatino was the closest thing Donati had to a son, he remembered telling Gabrielle. And as a memory had struggled to surface, she'd changed the subject with an abrupt question that had instantly set him thinking in an entirely different direction. He hadn't even noticed that she'd done it.

But now, underneath the soft, erotic swamping of his senses, the half-buried memory that had plagued him afterward crystalized. Like a silent freight train rushing out of the darkness, it slammed into his mind with headlines screaming. Vito Donati. Franco Sabatino. Donati's daughter, Sabatino's fiancée, dead in a fall from her second-story window.

Only she wasn't dead.

Devlin looked at the woman who lay sleeping so innocently beside him. Mafia princess Gabriela Donati was in bed with him. And he'd been suckered by the mistress of manipulation, the Queen of Sharks herself.

Devlin was gone when Gabrielle woke up. She sensed it even before she opened her eyes to the sunlight filtering in through the venetian blinds. It was fitting, she thought. The night was over. Time to face the music.

An hour later she stood in his office, waiting for him. He came in a few minutes after she arrived, a manila file folder tucked underneath his arm. "A little early, aren't you, Counselor?" he said. "The meeting with Sid's not for another half hour."

She stared at him for a moment before she remembered. "I'd forgotten that. Can we talk?"

"Confession time, is it?" he asked dryly. His sardonic gaze raked her up and down. Taking a seat, he waved his hand at a chair.

Gabrielle locked the door and faced him. His eyes, usually so warm with laughter and affection, were cold and cynical. Reclining in his chair, he waited for her to speak with that flinty gaze pinned on her. Why, she wondered, was he looking at her like that, before she'd said a word?

She crossed the room to stand in front of his desk. This wasn't her lover of the night before, or even her colleague of the past weeks. Judge and jury sat before her, but she had no miracles to pull out of her repertoire.

"I've kept something from you," she said. "Something important. I'm not who you think I am."

One corner of his mouth lifted, but it wasn't a

smile. "No? So tell me, *Gabriela*, who do I think you are?"

Her breath caught in her throat. Her heart all but stopped beating. "What—what did you call me?" Weak-kneed, she sank into a chair.

Devlin opened the manila folder he'd brought into the room and tossed it down in front of her. Page after page of photocopied newspaper articles spilled across his desk. Clippings about Vito Donati, Gabriela Donati, and Franco Sabatino. Reports, speculations regarding Gabriela Donati's supposed death. There were no photos of her, Vito had seen to that. But Devlin hadn't needed photos, she knew. The evidence was overwhelming. And totally damning.

"I've got to hand it to you," he said, tapping his finger on one particularly lurid clipping. "You're better than I ever imagined." His voice was deep, jeering. "Picture my surprise when I realized I'd been suckered by a master. No, better make that mistress. You must have really gotten off on that part of it."

Her stomach heaved, bile rising in her throat. "No! Devlin, that's not the way it was." She clutched his arm, sinking her fingers into it, imploring him to listen. "I love you. I wanted to tell you, but I—I couldn't."

Disgust etched in harsh lines on his face, Devlin shook his head. "You played me like that piano of yours. You even warned me, told me you were good." He bit out the words. "I can't argue with that. You're damned good, sweetheart. After all, you took me in, and God only knows with Celine as a prior, I knew better." He glanced at her hand on his arm, then his coldly furious gaze lifted to her face. "Did it sweeten the victory when I told you I'd fallen in love with you?"

She had known what his reaction would be, but that didn't make his anger and loathing any easier to bear. Sickened, she realized that her actions the night before had made things worse, if possible. Dropping her hand away, she said, "Oh, God, if I'd told you last night—"

"Yeah." His derisive laughter grated as he leaned across the desk, close enough to touch her, though he didn't. His voice dropped, took on an even more dangerous edge. "Last night was a great touch. I've been seduced by the best. Too bad there's always a morning after. The confession loses its effectiveness when the patsy knows he's been screwed. Doesn't it, *Gabriela*?"

"Don't call me that." She passed a shaky hand over her brow. If he would only listen, just for a moment. He would still hate her, but . . . "Let me explain. Please. You don't understand. Devlin, I couldn't tell you at first. I couldn't risk anyone knowing my real identity. When I left, I cut all my ties with my father and that way of life. I hadn't seen Franco in fourteen years. I was scared to death he'd expose me and then—"

"And then you wouldn't be in the sweet seat here, would you?" he interrupted. "No law partnership, no career taking off into the stratosphere, no nothing."

"At first, that was true, but it was never all of it. It wasn't just my career. Do you know what would happen if anyone—if the Mafia knew I was alive? Vito still has enemies within the organization. They'd love to kill me to get to him."

Devlin sat back and smiled at her, a mockery of the kind of smile he used to give her. "I don't deny your logic. It all makes sense. Perfectly logical, perfectly reasonable, the kind of work you'd expect from one of the best and brightest legal minds practicing today."

Oh God, he didn't believe her, he'd never believe her. He couldn't even hear her, he was so furious. She jumped up and strode around his desk, wanting to jerk him up from that chair and shake him until he listened to her. Instead she gripped the arms of his chair and glared at him, her face inches from his. "Do you really believe that you mean nothing to me? That I planned all this in order to get the partnership? That I slept with you to—to further my plans?"

He rose, forcing her away until she was backed up against the wall. His expression was as unreadable as a granite boulder and just as immobile. He traced a hand down her cheek to her shoulder, then palmed her breast, crudely. She swore and knocked his hand away, but not before she knew he'd felt her involuntary reaction to his touch and seen the flush rising in her face.

"I think you slept with me because you knew as well as I did that the sex would be great." He smiled thinly. "You weren't faking all those moans of pleasure, were you, sweetheart? But it sure as hell didn't hurt to have me under your thumb, did it? As for the rest of it—"

He broke off and gazed at her, his eyes looking like chips of ice, and his voice when he spoke was colder than a glacier. "I think you orchestrated the whole thing, every single minute, to play out just like you wanted it to. You wrote the score, you played the music. It was a virtuoso performance, *Gabriela*."

Only pride, what tiny portion she had left, kept her head high. "You're wrong, Devlin. Someday I hope you realize that."

He shook his head and gave a humorless laugh. "No, I'm not wrong. You figured to have me so bedazzled by your—how did Sabatino put it? Oh, yes, your *charms*, that I wouldn't have the time or energy left to go for the glory. And baby, it worked. All you had to do was bat those gorgeous eyes at me and say pretty please and I handed you the case, not to mention a damn good shot at the partnership, on a platter."

She gaped at him. He thought she'd asked to present the dismissal to further her career. Thought she'd used him, duped him—and the damnable thing was, she could see how it might look that way to him. At a loss for words, she only shook her head.

"I may be a slow learner, but I do learn," he said. "Eventually." He glanced at his watch, then strode to the door, opened it, and motioned for her to go through. "It's time to meet Sid. Come on, Counselor. I'll walk with you to his office."

In silence, Gabrielle followed him down the hall, wondering how she could still function when her heart was no longer beating.

Damn, she's good, Devlin thought bitterly, glancing at Gabrielle as they waited for Sid. The too-bright eyes, trembling lips, the pain that quivered in her voice—he could still almost buy the act. And the utter hell of it, the insult to all the injuries, was that even knowing what he did, he was still in love with her.

"Ah, glad you two are here," Sid said, breezing in. "I've just got a minute. Damned secretary scheduled a conflicting appointment." He fussed for a moment, pouring a cup of coffee, then took his place behind his desk.

Elbows on the desktop, fingers steepled, he spoke. "First, let me congratulate both of you on the Sabatino case. That went very well. Very well indeed."

Neither Devlin nor Gabrielle spoke. In fact, Devlin wondered if Gabrielle had even heard, so vacant was her expression.

Sid cleared his throat and continued. "As you both may know from the rumor mill, I've been contemplating early retirement. In this case, the rumors are true. I've been considering my successor, and I've come to a decision." Rising, he held out a hand to Gabrielle. "Gabrielle, I think you'll make a fine chief attorney of criminal defense litigation. Congratulations."

It wanted only this, Devlin thought, for the perfect ending. Gabrielle stared at Sid, looking totally stunned. My God, what an artist, he thought, even able to admire her in an odd, detached way. She'd won everything—just as she'd intended to all along.

Sid cleared his throat. "Gabrielle?"

"You want me to—?" She broke off, the epitome of confusion and surprise, and finally shook Sid's hand.

Devlin felt like putting his fist through something, but he was damned if he'd let her see him lose control. He'd lost before, been shafted before, but never quite so thoroughly. It was poetically, ironically perfect. What else had he expected when he took on the Queen of Sharks?

"Why don't we meet around three and discuss some details, Gabrielle?" Sid said. "I've got to run now." At the door, he paused. "By the way, I heard on the radio this morning that Franco Sabatino was murdered last night. Gunned down in front of a Deep Ellum bar about two A.M. Didn't have long to enjoy his freedom, did he?"

The door closed behind Sid, and silence hung in the room.

Gabrielle stared at the door, seemingly in shock. Devlin began to clap. "Wrapped up all neat and tidy," he said, shaking his head. "You're amazing."

Her brow furrowed as she looked at him. "What are you talking about?"

Devlin lifted an eyebrow. "Must be nice having a daddy who can off anybody who gives you problems."

"You think I—you think my father did this?" she asked incredulously.

"Come on, *Gabriela*, give me some credit. I know it wasn't you, since you happened to be seducing me about that time last night. But you ordered the hit."

Anger overrode the shock in her expression. She jumped to her feet and glared at him. "Do you really believe I ordered a hit on a man? On *anyone*, even Franco Sabatino?"

Devlin shrugged and rose. "Maybe not in so many words. Are you going to tell me you didn't call your father?"

"I—" Her gaze faltered, dropped. She turned her back on him and strode away a few steps. Still with her back to him, she spoke. "Vito didn't do it. He swore he wouldn't kill him."

"So you admit you talked to Donati." His hands fisted in his pockets. A part of him had wanted her to deny it, and would have believed her if she had. God, what a sap he was.

Whirling around, she shouted, "Yes, I talked to

him! I had to! Franco was about to—" Abruptly, she broke off. "I asked Vito to muzzle Franco, but he gave me his word he wouldn't kill him."

"The word of a Mafia don," Devlin said scornfully.

"My father's word," she said, her head held high and her green eyes colder than a winter's dawn. "You know nothing about him, and obviously, nothing about me either. Vito kept his word to me for fourteen years. I won't start doubting him now. He didn't order that hit."

His mouth curved into a satiric smile. "Mighty convenient of Sabatino to go get himself shot, wasn't it?"

"Do you think Franco didn't have other enemies? He's bound to have had scores of them."

"Why did they pick now to kill him, then? Why not last week or last year? Or a month from now?"

"I don't know." She took an agitated turn and faced him again. "This is—this probably is my fault, in part. All Vito had to do was put the word out that Franco was no longer in his favor. It would be enough to get him killed."

"You are so damned good, it's unbelievable. Congratulations, Counselor. How does it feel to have it all? Promotion, probable partnership, money, the glory. And no Sabatino to threaten it."

She said nothing, simply looked at him blankly. Unable to bear more, Devlin strode to the door. "Of course, you'll have to find another lover," he added, turning to make one last jab, "but I don't imagine it will take long to break in a new one. Not for a woman of your—" He paused and added with an ironical lift of his eyebrow—"talents."

Her gaze met his. He'd never seen a bleaker expression in anyone's eyes. "If that's what you believe," she said, "what you honestly believe, then there's nothing more I can say to you."

"Not unless it's *Arrivederci*, sucker," Devlin said, and walked out.

FIFTEEN

"Mr. Norris wants you in his office, Mr. Sinclair," Devlin's secretary told him when he came in the next morning.

"Later." He wasn't doing anything that didn't involve aspirin and dim light.

She rose from her desk and walked toward him, holding out a pile of messages. "He says it's urgent."

Ignoring her, Devlin shut the door in her face. The last thing he needed was to see Sid. The night before he'd gone home and, lacking a better course of action, had gotten drunk. Stumbling, knee-walking drunk. Not that it had done him any good. He could still remember every detail of every moment he'd spent with Gabrielle. And every detail of yesterday's revelations.

His intercom buzzed. He swore and considered shoving the phone off the desk. The annoying noise continued until he snatched the receiver up and bellowed, "What?" into it. Wincing, he reminded himself not to shout when he had a hangover.

"Mr. Norris just called again," the secretary said, and sniffed. "I told him you hadn't arrived yet."

Her disapproval was clear from her frigid tone. Devlin swore silently and gave up, knowing he'd be badgered until he took care of it. "I'm going."

Five minutes later he strode into Sid's office. "You needed to see me?"

"Have a seat, Sinclair. Coffee?" At Devlin's nod, he poured him a cup, handed it to him. Devlin immediately wondered what Sid was up to. The man wasn't generally so solicitous.

"I tried to get you yesterday afternoon, but you'd left for the day." Sid hesitated, sipped his coffee, fiddled with his watch. "Let me be blunt," he finally said. "How would you like to be chief attorney of criminal defense litigation when I retire?"

Devlin stared at him. What the hell was going on? "Doesn't Gabrielle have something to say about that? You offered the same position to her just yesterday as I recall."

"Yes, ah, I know." His pasty complexion reddened. "The thing is, she turned it down."

Turned it down? "Gabrielle turned down the promotion?"

Sid nodded. "Yesterday afternoon, when I met

with her again. Not only turned the position down, but she's resigned from CG and S. Effective immediately."

Devlin could think of no reason why Gabrielle would turn down that promotion. Or why she would resign. It made no sense. Quit, just when she'd gotten the very thing she'd been scheming for?

"I thought you might know something about her decision," Sid continued.

"No. Nothing." What did it mean? Had she quit because she thought he'd expose her?

"Too bad. I don't mind telling you it was the weirdest thing I ever experienced. She came in here, said she was sorry but she couldn't work here anymore, handed in her resignation, and was gone. Took her all of a minute." He frowned and added petulantly, "Didn't even give two weeks' notice. Just up and quit."

Sid continued talking, but Devlin didn't listen. He was too busy trying to figure out Gabrielle's game. She must think he was going to tell Sid about her background. It was the only reason he could come up with that explained her behavior. If that was her reasoning, though, all she had to do was call in her father and Devlin wouldn't be a threat.

But she wouldn't do that, he admitted. Just as he'd known, even as he accused her of it, that she hadn't ordered a hit on Franco Sabatino. No matter how ambitious she was, he knew she wasn't capable of ordering a man's death. He'd said it because he was angry. Because he was hurt. Because she'd made him fall for her and prove himself a fool.

Sid's voice penetrated his thoughts. "Well? What do you say?"

Pulled out of his reverie, Devlin glanced at him. "About what?"

Exasperated, Sid repeated, "The position, man. Haven't you heard anything I've been saying?"

No, Devlin thought, but he didn't tell Sid that. "I'll have to think about it. The fact that I'm your second choice doesn't do a lot for me."

Sid flushed again. "Dammit, Sinclair, you can't hold that against us. Think of your career."

He intended to. In fact, he intended to think long and hard about a lot of things. "I'll let you know."

A week later, Devlin still hadn't made up his mind. He went to work every day and tried to decide why he felt none of the old excitement, none of the anticipation he used to feel at the prospect of a new case, a new challenge. He'd been offered the plum position, a chance at partnership. Everything he'd wanted and intended to have. Why didn't he accept Sid's offer and get on with it?

There was a new clerk in the corporate department who'd been giving him the eye. She was blonde, beautiful, eager. And Devlin didn't feel even a flicker of interest. Nothing. Not lust, not desire, not even mild appreciation. Rather, he felt drained, as vacant and empty as a dead man's eyes. Damn Gabrielle, he thought. She'd messed with his head even worse than she had messed with his career. No woman since Celine had hurt him so badly, and he suspected that much of his pain then had sprung from hurt pride.

With Gabrielle it wasn't his pride that hurt. Dammit, she'd broken his heart. Or he had broken it himself when he let her go.

Every time he walked into the law library he could see her poring over her work, her dark hair gleaming in the soft lamplight. He could see her taking off those horn-rimmed glasses, giving him a better look at those gorgeous green eyes. Or he'd pass by her office and see her desk, and remember what she'd looked like the night they'd made love in there.

He couldn't listen to the classical music station on the radio without wanting to throw something. He couldn't sleep worth crap because often as not, she was in his dreams. And if he wasn't dreaming about making love with her, he was dreaming about the bleak, hopeless expression in her eyes the last time he saw her. That was worse. Much, much worse. Dammit, she was ruining his life, and she wasn't even in it anymore.

She'd set up a law office not too far from CG&S. A few streets over, in a cheaper section of town. Apparently, she and Nina still kept in touch, because he'd overheard Nina talking about it. Gabrielle had made no effort to contact him. But why would she, after everything he'd said to her?

But what about what she'd done to him? She'd lied, though he could hardly fault her for that. At least at first. But after they'd become lovers she could have told him. Could have at least tried . . . But he wouldn't have been any more understanding, he knew. The idea that she'd played him for a fool would have taken hold and he wouldn't have listened to her, no matter when she told him or what her explanation was.

He'd been wrong about Gabrielle, just as he'd been wrong about Donati. A few days earlier the circumstances surrounding Sabatino's death had come out. The man in custody for the murder was not connected with Donati in any way. So she hadn't been lying about that, either.

Devlin swung his chair around to gaze out his window. Not as good a view of the Dallas skyline as Sid's office presented, but he could remedy that soon. If he wanted to. He could have everything; it was there for the taking. Everything he'd thought he wanted, and nothing he now knew he needed.

Because none of it meant a damn thing if Gabrielle wasn't there to share it with him.

One more wall down, Gabrielle thought with satisfaction, laying the paint roller in the nearly empty tray. Not a bad job, especially considering she was no painter. Absently, she wiped her hands on the back of her cutoffs. So what if she'd put nearly as much paint in her hair and on her clothes as on the office walls? It was looking good. Another couple of days and she'd be ready to open. Her new office wasn't impressive, but it was functional. And it was all hers. She'd hung out her shingle that morning: Gabrielle Rousseau, Attorney-at-law.

She was happy, she decided. Maybe not ecstatically happy, but she was at peace. With her father, with her career, with herself. If there was a huge, gaping hole in her life, she would soon have enough work to fill it. In time she would succeed, she knew that. And she would work with the clients she wanted to work with, clients she chose to work with. She was in charge of her own destiny now, and she found she liked it very much.

But Lord, she missed Devlin so much at times, she could hardly breathe for the pain. She was surviving, but she wondered if the ache would ever dull. What was he doing? Had he already moved into Sid's office? Nina hadn't said so, but after Gabrielle had bitten her head off the first few times Nina had mentioned Devlin, she'd quit talking about him.

Was he happy? Did he miss her?

Right. Somehow she couldn't picture Devlin moping around with a broken heart. He was a lot more likely to find some gorgeous babe to help him heal it. And there were plenty of those around when the man in question was Devlin Sinclair.

Gabrielle didn't blame him for hating her. Not much. But she did blame him for believing that she'd had Franco killed. That had hurt. Had they known each other at all? If they had, how could he believe her capable of ordering a man's death?

It's over, she thought, *so quit torturing yourself*. She moved the ladder, picked up the paint can, and started refilling the tray.

"Nice digs," a voice said from the doorway.

The can jerked, spattering paint on the ladder, the drop cloth, and her legs. Devlin's voice. The sound of it swept through her, giving her sudden joy, followed by a mix of feelings ranging from pain to happiness. Her heart thudded so loudly, she could hardly think. Carefully, she set the can down and turned to face him.

For a long moment she studied him, drinking in the sight of him. He looked as good as ever, with the sleeves of his baby-blue dress shirt rolled up and that knock-em-dead smile on his face, but she thought his eyes looked strained. Maybe he *had* missed her. "I like it," she said, wondering how she could sound so calm.

Hands stuffed in the pockets of his navy slacks, he strolled in and looked around. "So, how's business?"

Unsure of his motive for being there, she simply stared at him. He expected her to make small talk, she thought, when all she could hear were the echoes of their last conversation? Bitter, hurtful, angry words. And though she understood his feelings, she couldn't pretend the words had never been said. But it was his move, so she answered him in kind.

"Not open yet," she said, raising her chin and meeting his gaze. "How's CG and S?"

He shrugged and didn't speak, taking another turn around the room before he halted in front of her. Reaching out, he touched her cheek, then cupped it. "You've got paint on your face."

For an instant, she closed her eyes, and her breath drew in at his touch. "I've got paint everywhere," she managed to say, with a creditable attempt at nonchalance.

His hand lingered when she started to move away, then his other one came up to frame her face. "God, I've missed you," he said.

She saw the truth of it in his eyes. He really had missed her, and God knows, she'd missed him too. Unable to speak, she gazed at him with a lump the size of Texas lodged in her throat. When she didn't move, he leaned forward and she knew he was going to kiss her. Quickly, she jerked her face away and backed up a step, nearly turning over the paint tray in the process. Kissing him would solve nothing. It would only hurt her more because she still didn't know why he was there.

"What do you want, Devlin?" Retreating to the window, she strove desperately for balance, for calm as she asked the question, but she could hear the quaver in her voice, and she knew he could too.

"That's the same question I've been asking my-

self. And I think I finally figured out the answer."
His gaze locked with hers. "I want you, Gabrielle."

He wanted her. But then, sex had never been the problem between them. She didn't answer.

He took a step forward and spoke again. "I want you back."

Wanted her back? Just like that? With no discussion, no nothing? Was she supposed to fall into his arms simply because he snapped his fingers? After the things he'd said, and worse, the things he thought her capable of?

Her expression hardened. "Really?" she asked sarcastically. "I'm the same woman you accused just a week ago of having Sabatino murdered. The same woman you think betrayed you to further her career, the same woman—"

"The woman I'm in love with," he interrupted. "The woman I never believed ordered Sabatino's death."

Damn, his voice made his words sound so convincing. She ought to be used to it, after years of hearing lawyers speak. "You certainly gave a good impression of believing it."

"I was hurt. Angry. I lashed out." He frowned and threw a hand up in the air. "Hell, Gabrielle, what did you expect? It blew me away when I realized who you were. And then after Sid offered you the promotion—"

"You automatically assumed that because my father is Mafia, that I must operate the same way."

He rammed his fingers through his hair. "You'd

been lying to me for weeks. Lying from the minute we met. It didn't inspire a lot of confidence, no matter how much I *wanted* to believe you were different. No matter how much I wanted to believe you had a good reason for what you were doing."

Turning her back, she gazed out the window. She should have told him the truth that last night, if not before. But she'd been afraid of what the truth would do, so she hadn't.

"I've been thinking," he said. "Hell, I haven't done anything *but* think for the past week. If making partner had been your only goal, than you'd never have quit CG and S. If you'd been the woman I accused you of being, you'd never have quit. And I knew, deep down, that you weren't that woman."

Admitting that she was to blame as well wasn't easy. Her back still toward him, she said, "You had good reason to feel the way you did."

"It doesn't matter anymore."

"Yes, it does." She faced him. "Are you ever going to trust me? When you know I lied?"

"I also know *why* you lied. That makes a difference." He closed the distance between them and slipped his arms around her waist, pulling her near, resting his cheek against hers. Hesitant at first, she put her hands on his arms. His breath felt warm, wafting across her cheek. Closing her eyes, she savored the sensation.

His voice was deep and quiet when he spoke. "I kept going to work, thinking about the position, the partnership. I should have been happy, but I wasn't. I'd gotten everything I wanted, but none of it meant a damn to me because I'd lost you. Come back to me, Gabrielle." He paused, then said, "I love you."

She opened her eyes and looked into his, seeing the love in them. It hurt to throw up more objections, when all she wanted was to fall into his arms. "I'm not sure you understand what you'd be getting into. My past might always haunt me. Franco threatened to kill you. It could happen again, if someone else found out."

He was smiling at her, that smile she loved so much. Didn't he understand what she was saying?

"You called your father for me, didn't you? I'd wondered what made you do it then, instead of when Franco first showed up."

She nodded. "I won't do it again. The only reason I did it was because I had no other choice. I'm not Gabriela Donati. I never will be again. I'm a different person now. Gabrielle Rousseau."

"I've never known you as anyone else. I love you, Gabrielle."

"I love you too, Devlin."

He kissed her then, the sweetest, most tender kiss she thought she'd ever had. For a long time, they stood there holding each other until finally Devlin pulled back to look at her, keeping his arms around her.

"If you wanted to come back to CG and S, Sid would still give you the job."

"No." She shook her head and smiled at him. "I've discovered that's not what I want after all. I'm happy going into practice by myself."

"Good. I'm glad that was your answer." He grinned. "How about a partner?"

"You mean—?"

He nodded. "I resigned this morning. What do you say, Counselor? Think you could stomach me as a partner?"

"I think I might manage it," she said, smiling. "We work really well together."

"In more ways than one. And I know just the way to celebrate our upcoming partnership."

Since he'd slid his hands inside her cutoffs and was massaging her rear while he kissed her, she had a good idea of what he intended. "The desk isn't here yet," she murmured against his lips.

"That's okay. We'll improvise." He kissed her again. "There's one more thing."

In the process of unbuttoning his shirt, she paused. "What?"

He covered her hands with both of his. "Marry me, Gabrielle."

Stunned, she stammered, "Y-you want to get married?" Oh, that smile should definitely be licensed, she thought.

"Yes." He brought her hands to his lips and kissed them, watching her with a devilish gleam in his eyes. "Say yes."

"We haven't known each other very long. We don't have to rush into it." Even though she realized there was nothing she'd like more than to marry him, she felt compelled to give him an out.

"Yes we do." He clasped her hands together at his chest. "I've been going crazy without you. I want to be with you, all the time. Marry me and put me out of my misery."

"When you put it like that, what other choice do I have?" She smiled and curved her arms around his neck. "Yes," she said, and kissed him to seal it.

THE EDITORS' CORNER

Men. We love 'em, we hate 'em, but when it comes right down to it, we can't get along without 'em. Especially the ones we may never meet: those handsome guys with the come-hither eyes, those gentle giants with the hearts of gold, those debonair men who make you want to say yes. Well, this October you'll get your chance to meet those very men. Their stories make up LOVESWEPT's MEN OF LEGEND month. There's nothing like reuniting with an old flame, and the men our four authors have picked will definitely have you shivering with delight!

Marcia Evanick presents the final chapter in her White Lace & Promises trilogy, **HERE'S LOOKIN' AT YOU**, LOVESWEPT #854. Morgan De Witt promised his father that he would take care of his sister, Georgia. Now that Georgia's happily engaged, he's facing a lonely future and has decided it's time to find a Mrs. De Witt. Enter Maddie Andrews. Years ago, Maddie offered Morgan her heart, and he rebuffed the gawky fifteen-year-old. Morgan can't understand why Maddie is so aloof, but he's determined to crack her defenses, even if he has to send her the real Maltese Falcon to do so. Maddie's heart melts every time he throws in a line or two from her favorite actor, but can she overcome the fears bedeviling her every thought of happiness? As usual, Marcia Evanick delights readers with a love that is at times difficult, but always, always enduring.

Loveswept favorite Sandra Chastain returns with **MAC'S ANGELS: SCARLET LADY,** LOVE-SWEPT #855. Rhett Butler Montana runs his riverboat casino like the rogue he was named for, but when a mysterious woman in red breaks the bank and then dares him to play her for everything he owns, he's sorely tempted to abandon his Southern gentility in favor of a little one-on-one. With her brother missing and her family's plantation at stake, Katie Carithers has her own agenda in mind; she must form an uneasy alliance with the gambler who's bound by honor to help any damsel in distress. As the two battle over integrity, family, and loyalty, Katie and Rhett discover that what matters most is not material but intangible—that thing called love. Sandra Chastain ignites a fiery duel of wits and wishes when she sends a sexy rebel to do battle with his leading lady.

Next up is Stephanie Bancroft's delightful tale of Kat McKray and James Donovan, the former British agent who boasts a **LICENSE TO THRILL,** LOVESWEPT #856. Even though James Donovan is known the world over as untouchable and hard to hold, he has never lacked for companionship of the female persuasion. But after delivering a letter of historic consequence to the curvaceous museum curator, James is sure his sacred state of bachelorhood is doomed. Kat refuses to lose her heart to another love 'em and leave 'em kind of guy, a vow that slowly dissolves in the wake of James's presence. When Kat is arrested in the disappearance of the valuable artifact, it's up to James to save Kat's reputation and find the true culprit. In a romantic caper that taps into every woman's fantasy of 007 in hot pursuit, Stephanie keeps the pulse racing with a woman desperate to clear her name and that of the spy who loves her.

Talk about a tall tale! Donna Kauffman delivers **LIGHT MY FIRE**, LOVESWEPT #857, a novel about a smoke jumper and a maverick agent whose strength and determination are matched only by each other's. Larger than life, 6′ 7″ T. J. Delahaye rescues people for a living and enjoys it. By no means a shrinking violet at 6′ 2″, Jenna King rescues the environment and is haunted by it. But you know what they say—the bigger they are, the harder they fall—and these two are no exception. Trapped by the unrelenting forces of nature, Jenna and T. J. must rely on instinct and each other to survive. Sorrow has touched them both deeply, and if they make it through this ordeal alive, will they put aside the barriers long enough to learn the secret thrill of surrender? In a story fiercely erotic and deeply moving, Donna draws the reader into an inferno of emotion and fans the flames high with the heat of heartbreaking need.

Happy reading!

With warmest regards,

Susann Brailey   *Joy Abella*

Susann Brailey   Joy Abella

Senior Editor   Administrative Editor

P.S. Look for these Bantam women's fiction titles coming in October. From Jane Feather, Patricia Coughlin, Sharon & Tom Curtis, Elizabeth Elliott, Patricia Potter, and Suzanne Robinson comes **WHEN YOU WISH . . .** , a collection of truly romantic tales, in which a mysterious bottle containing one wish falls into the hands of each of the heroines . . . with magical results. Hailed by *Romantic Times* as "an exceptional talent with a tremendous gift for involving her readers in the story," Jane Ashford weaves a historical romance between Ariel Harding and the Honorable Alan Gresham, an unlikely alliance that will lead to the discovery of a dark truth and unexpected love in **THE BARGAIN**. National bestselling author Kay Hooper intertwines the lives of two women, strangers who are drawn together by one fatal moment, in **AFTER CAROLINE**. Critically acclaimed author Glenna McReynolds offers us **THE CHALICE AND THE BLADE**, the romantic fantasy of Ceridwen and Dain, struggling to escape the dangers and snares set by friend and foe alike, while discovering that neither can resist the love that promises to bind them forever. And immediately following this page, take a sneak peek at the Bantam women's fiction titles on sale in August.

DARK PARADISE
by **Tami Hoag**

Here is nationally bestselling author Tami Hoag's breathtakingly sensual novel, a story filled with heart-stopping suspense and shocking passion . . . a story of a woman drawn to a man as hard and untamable as the land he loves, and to a town steeped in secrets—where a killer lurks.

She could hear the dogs in the distance, baying relentlessly. Pursuing relentlessly, as death pursues life.

Death.

Christ, she was going to die. The thought made her incredulous. Somehow, she had never really believed this moment would come. The idea had always loitered in the back of her mind that she would somehow be able to cheat the grim reaper, that she would be able to deal her way out of the inevitable. She had always been a gambler. Somehow, she had always managed to beat the odds. Her heart fluttered and her throat clenched at the idea that she would not beat them this time.

The whole notion of her own mortality stunned her, and she wanted to stop and stare at herself, as if she were having an out-of-body experience, as if this person running were someone she knew only in passing. But she couldn't stop. The sounds of the dogs drove her on. The instinct of self-preservation spurred her to keep her feet moving.

She lunged up the steady grade of the mountain, tripping over exposed roots and fallen branches. Brush grabbed her clothing and clawed her bloodied face like gnarled, bony fingers. The carpet of decay on the forest floor gave way in spots as she scrambled, yanking her back precious inches instead of giving her purchase to propel herself forward. Pain seared through her as her elbow cracked against a stone half buried in the soft loam. She picked herself up, cradling the arm against her body, and ran on.

Sobs of frustration and fear caught in her throat and choked her. Tears blurred what sight she had in the moon-silvered night. Her nose was broken and throbbing, forcing her to breathe through her mouth alone, and she tried to swallow the cool night air in great gulps. Her lungs were burning, as if every breath brought in a rush of acid instead of oxygen. The fire spread down her arms and legs, limbs that felt like leaden clubs as she pushed them to perform far beyond their capabilities.

I should have quit smoking. A ludicrous thought. It wasn't cigarettes that was going to kill her. In an isolated corner of her mind, where a strange calm resided, she saw herself stopping and sitting down on a fallen log for a final smoke. It would have been like those nights after aerobics class, when the first thing she had done outside the gym was light up. Nothing like that first smoke after a workout. She laughed, on the verge of hysteria, then sobbed, stumbled on.

The dogs were getting closer. They could smell the blood that ran from the deep cut the knife had made across her face.

There was no one to run to, no one to rescue her. She knew that. Ahead of her, the terrain only turned more rugged, steeper, wilder. There were no people, no roads. There was no hope.

Her heart broke with the certainty of that. No hope. Without hope, there was nothing. All the other systems began shutting down.

She broke from the woods and stumbled into a clearing. She couldn't run another step. Her head swam and pounded. Her legs wobbled beneath her, sending her lurching drunkenly into the open meadow. The commands her brain sent shorted out en route, then stopped firing altogether as her will crumbled.

Strangling on despair, on the taste of her own blood, she sank to her knees in the deep, soft grass and stared up at the huge, brilliant disk of the moon, realizing for the first time in her life how insignificant she was. She would die in this wilderness, with the scent of wildflowers in the air, and the world would go on without a pause. She was nothing, just another victim of another hunt. No one would even miss her. The sense of stark loneliness that thought sent through her numbed her to the bone.

No one would miss her.

No one would mourn her.

Her life meant nothing.

She could hear the crashing in the woods behind her. The sound of hoofbeats. The snorting of a horse. The dogs baying. Her heart pounding, ready to explode.

She never heard the shot.

FROM THE *New York Times* BESTSELLING

BETINA KRAHN

With the wit of *The Last Bachelor*, the charm of *The Perfect Mistress*, and the sparkle of *The Unlikely Angel*, Betina Krahn has penned an enchanting new romance

THE MERMAID

If Celeste Ashton hadn't needed money to save her grandmother's seaside estate, she would never have published her observations on ocean life and the dolphins she has befriended. So when her book makes her an instant celebrity, she is unprepared for the attention . . . especially when it comes from unnervingly handsome Titus Thorne. While Titus suspects there is something fishy about her theories, Celeste is determined to be taken seriously. Soon their fiery ideological clashes create sparks neither expects, and Titus must decide if he will risk his credibility, his career—and his heart—to side with the Lady Mermaid.

"KRAHN HAS A DELIGHTFUL, SMART TOUCH."
—*Publishers Weekly*

"Miss Ashton, permit me to apologize for what may appear to one outside the scientific community to be rudeness on the part of our members. We are all accustomed to the way the vigorous spirit of inquiry often leads to enthusiastic questioning and debate. The familiarity of long acquaintance and the dogged pursuit of truth sometimes lead us to overstep the bounds of general decorum."

She stared at the tall, dark-haired order bringer, uncertain whether to be irritated or grateful that he had just taken over her lecture.

"I believe I . . . understand."

Glancing about the lecture hall, she was indeed beginning to understand. She had received their invitation to speak as an honor, and had prepared her lecture under the assumption that she was being extended a coveted offer of membership in the societies. But, in fact, she had not been summoned here to *join;* she had been summoned here to *account*. They had issued her an invitation to an inquisition . . . for the grave offense of publishing research without the blessing of the holy orders of science: the royal societies.

"Perhaps if I restated a few of the questions I have heard put forward just now," he said, glancing at the members seated around him, "it would preserve order and make for a more productive exchange."

Despite his handsome smile and extreme mannerliness, her instincts warned that here was no ally.

"You state that most of your observations have been made while you were in the water with the creatures, themselves." As he spoke, he made his way to the end of the row, where the others in the aisle made way for him to approach the front of the stage.

"That is true," she said, noting uneasily the way the others parted for him.

"If I recall correctly, you stated that you sail or row out into the bay waters, rap out a signal on the hull of your boat, and the dolphin comes to greet you. You then slip into the water with the creature—or creatures, if he has brought his family group—hold your breath, and dive under the water to observe them."

"That is precisely what happens. Though I must say, it is a routine perfected by extreme patience and long experience. Years, in fact."

"You expect us to believe you not only call these creatures at will, but that you voluntarily . . . single-handedly . . . climb into frigid water with any number of these monstrous large beasts, and that you swim underwater for hours on end to observe them?" He straightened, glancing at the others as he readied his thrust. "That is a great deal indeed to believe on the word of a young woman who has no scientific training and no formal academic background."

His words struck hard and sank deep. So that was it. She was young and female and intolerably presumptuous to attempt to share her learning and experiences with the world when she hadn't the proper credentials.

"It is true that I have had no formal academic training. But I studied and worked with my grandfather for years; learning the tenants of reason and logic, developing theoretical approaches, observing and recording." She stepped out from behind the podium, facing him, facing them all for the sake of what she knew to be the truth.

"There is much learning, sir, to be had *outside* the hallowed, ivy-covered walls of a university. Experience is a most excellent tutor."

She saw him stiffen as her words found a mark in him. But a moment later, all trace of that fleeting reaction was gone.

"Very well, Miss Ashton, let us proceed and see what your particular brand of science has produced." His words were now tightly clipped, tailored for maximum impact. "You observe underwater, do you not? Just how do you *see* all of these marvels several yards beneath the murky surface?"

"Firstly, ocean water is not 'murky.' Anyone who has spent time at the seaside knows that." She moved to the table and picked up a pair of goggles. "Secondly, I wear these. They are known in sundry forms to divers on various continents."

"Very well, it might work. But several obstacles still remain. Air, for instance. How could you possibly stay under the water long enough to have seen all that you report?"

She looked up at him through fiercely narrowed eyes.

"I hold my breath."

"Indeed? Just how long can you hold your breath, Miss Ashton?"

"Minutes at a time."

"Oh?" His eyebrows rose. "And what proof do you have?"

"Proof? What proof do you need?" she demanded, her hands curling into fists at her sides. "Shall I stick my head in a bucket for you?"

Laughter skittered through their audience, only to die when he shot them a censuring look. "Perhaps we could arrange an impromptu test of your remarkable breathing ability, Miss Ashton. I propose that you hold your breath—right here, right now—and we will time you."

"Don't be ridiculous," she said, feeling crowded by his height and intensity. He stood head and shoulders above her and obviously knew how to use his size to advantage in a confrontation.

"It is anything *but* ridiculous," he declared. "It would be a demonstration of the repeatability of a phenomenon. Repetition of results is one of the key tests of scientific truth, is it not?"

"It would not be a true trial," she insisted, but loathe to mention why. His silence and smug look combined with derogatory comments from the audience to prod it from her. "I am wearing a 'dress improver,'" she said through clenched teeth, "which restricts my breathing."

"Oh. Well." He slid his gaze down to her waist, allowing it to linger there for a second too long. When she glared at him, he smiled. "We can adjust for that by giving you . . . say . . . ten seconds?"

Before she could protest, he called for a mirror to detect stray breath. None could be found on such short notice, so, undaunted, he volunteered to hold a strip of paper beneath her nose to detect any intake of air. The secretary, Sir Hillary, was drafted as a timekeeper and a moment later she was forced to purge her lungs, strain her corset to take in as much air as possible, and then hold it.

Her inquisitor leaned close, holding that fragile strip of paper, watching for the slightest flutter in it. And as she struggled to find the calm center into which she always retreated while diving, she began to feel the heat radiating from him . . . the warmth of his face near her own . . . the energy coming from his broad shoulders. And she saw his eyes, mere inches from hers, beginning to wander over her face. Was he purposefully trying to distract her? Her quickening pulse said that if he was, his tactic was working. To combat it, she searched desperately for someplace to fasten her vision, something to concentrate on. Unfortunately, the closest available thing was *him*.

Green eyes, she realized, with mild surprise. Blue

green, really. The color of sunlight streaming into the sea on a midsummer day. His skin was firm and lightly tanned . . . stretched taut over a broad forehead, high cheekbones, and a prominent, slightly aquiline nose. Her gaze drifted downward to his mouth . . . full, velvety looking, with a prominent dip in the center of his upper lip that made his mouth into an intriguing bow. There were crinkle lines at the corners of his eyes and a beard shadow was forming along the edge of his cheek.

She found herself licking her lip . . . lost in the bold angles and intriguing textures of his very male face . . . straining for control and oblivious to the fact that half of the audience was on its feet and moving toward the stage. She had never observed a man this close for this long—well, besides her grandfather and the brigadier. A man. A handsome man. His hair was a dark brown, not black, she thought desperately. And as her chest began to hurt, she fastened her gaze on his eyes and held on with everything in her. This was for science. This was for her dolphins. This was to teach those sea green eyes a lesson . . .

The ache in her chest gradually crowded everything but him and his eyes from her consciousness. Finally, when she felt the dimming at the edges of her vision, which spelled real danger, she blew out that breath and then gasped wildly. The fresh air was so intoxicating that she staggered.

A wave of astonishment greeted the news that she had held her breath for a full three minutes.

BRIDE OF DANGER
by **Katherine O'Neal**

Winner of the *Romantic Times* Award for Best
Sensual Historical Romance

*Night after night, she graced London's most elegant
soirees, her flame-haired beauty drawing all eyes, her
innocent charm wresting from men the secrets of their
souls. And not one suspected the truth: that she was a
spy, plucked from the squalor of Dublin's filthy streets.
For Mylene, devoted to the cause of freedom, it was a
role she gladly played . . . until the evening she came
face-to-face with the mysterious Lord Whitney. All of the
ton was abuzz with his recent arrival. But only Mylene
knew he was as much of an imposter as she. Gone was
any trace of Johnny, the wild Irish youth she
remembered. In his place was a rogue more devastatingly
handsome than any man had a right to be—and a rebel
coldheartedly determined to do whatever it took to fulfill
his mission. Now he was asking Mylene to betray
everything she'd come to believe in. And even as she
knew she had to stop him, she couldn't resist
surrendering to his searing passion.*

On the boat to England, Mylene had learned her role.
She was to play an English orphan who'd lost her
parents in an Irish uprising and, for want of any rela-
tions, had been shipped home to an English orphan-
age. The story would explain Mylene's knowledge of
Dublin. But more, it was calculated to stir the embers
of her adoptive father Lord Stanley's heart. He was
the staunchest opposition Parliament had to Irish
Home Rule. That Mylene's parents had been killed

by Irish rabble rousers garnered his instant sympathy. He'd taken her in at first glance, and formally adopted her within the year.

In the beginning, Mylene had been flabbergasted by her surroundings. She wasn't certain she could perform such an extended role without giving herself away. The luxurious lifestyle, the formalities and graces, proved matters of extreme discomfort. To be awakened in the warmth of her plush canopied bed with a cup of steaming cocoa embarrassed her as much as being waited on hand and foot. But soon enough, James—the driver who secretly worked for their cause—had passed along her assignment. She was to use her position to discover the scandalous secrets of Lord Stanley's friends and associates. Buoyed by the sense of purpose, she'd thrown herself into her task with relish, becoming accomplished at the subterfuge in no time.

What she hadn't counted on was growing to love Lord Stanley. Ireland, and her old life, began to seem like the dream.

"How fares the Countess?" he asked, thinking she'd gone to visit a friend.

"Well enough, I think, for all that her confinement makes her edgy."

"Well, it's all to a good purpose, as she'll see when the baby comes. But tell me, my dear, did her happy state have its effect? I shouldn't mind a grandchild of my own before too much time."

"The very thing we were discussing when you came in," announced his companion.

Mylene turned and looked at Roger Helmsley. He was a dashing gentleman of thirty years, tall with dark brown hair and a fetching pencil-thin mustache. He wore his evening clothes with negligent ease, secure in his wealth and position. He was Lord Stanley's compatriot in Parliament, the driving force behind the Irish opposition.

"Lord Helmsley has been pressing his suit," explained her father. "He informs me, with the most dejected of countenances, that he's asked for your hand on three separate occasions. Yet he says you stall him with pretty smiles."

"She's a coy one, my lord," said Roger, coming to take both her hands in his. "I daresay some of your own impeccable diplomacy has rubbed off on your daughter."

"Is this a conspiracy?" she laughed. "Is a girl not to be allowed her say?"

"If you'd say anything at all, I might bear up. But this blasted silence on the subject . . . Come, my sweet. What must an old bachelor like myself do to entice the heart of such a fair maiden?"

Roger was looking at her with a glow of appreciation that to this day made her flush with wonder. At twenty-two, Mylene had blossomed under the Earl's care. The rich food from his table had transformed the scrawny street urchin into a woman with enticing curves. Her breasts were full, her hips ripe and rounded, her legs nicely lean and defined from hours in the saddle and long walks through Hyde Park. Her skin, once so sallow, glowed with rosy health. Even her riotous curls glistened with rich abundance. Her pouty mouth was legendary among the swells of Marlboro House. Her clothes were fashioned by the best dressmakers in London, giving her a regal, polished air—if one didn't look too closely at the impish scattering of freckles across her nose. But when she looked in the mirror, she always gave a start of surprise. She thought of herself still as the ill-nourished orphan without so much as a last name.

It was partly this quest for a family of her own that had her considering Roger's proposal. He was an affable and decent man who, on their outings, had displayed a free-wheeling sense of the absurd that had brought an element of fun to her sadly serious life. His wealth, good looks, and charm were the talk of mothers with marriageable daughters. And if his politics appalled her, she'd learned long ago from Lord Stanley that a man could hold differing, even dangerous political views, and still be the kindest of men. Admittedly, the challenge intrigued her. As his wife, she could perhaps influence him to take a more liberal stance.

"You see how she avoids me," Roger complained in a melodramatic tone.

There was a knock on the door before the panels were slid open by Jensen, the all-too-proper majordomo who'd been in the service of Lord Stanley's grandfather. "Excuse the intrusion, my lord, but a gentleman caller awaits your pleasure without."

"A caller?" asked Lord Stanley. "At this hour?"

"His card, my lord."

Lord Stanley took the card. "Good gracious. Lord Whitney. Send him in, Jensen, by all means."

When Jensen left with a stiff bow, Roger asked, "A jest perhaps? A visit from the grave?"

"No, no, my good man. Not old Lord Whitney. It's his son. I'd heard on his father's death that he was on his way. Been in India with his mother since he was a lad. As you know, the climate agreed with her, and she refused to return when her husband's service was at an end. Kept the boy with her. We haven't seen the scamp since he was but a babe."

"Well, well, this *is* news! It's our duty, then, to set

him straight right from the start. Curry his favor, so to speak. We shouldn't want the influence he's inherited to go the wrong way."

"He's his father's son. He'll see our way of things, I'll warrant."

Mylene knew what this meant. Old Lord Whitney, while ill and with one foot in the grave, had nevertheless roused himself to Parliament in his wheelchair to lambaste, in his raspy voice, the MPs who favored Ireland's pleas. Lord Stanley, she knew, was counting on the son to take up the cause. It meant another evening of feeling her hackles rise as the gentlemen discussed new ways to squelch the Irish rebellion.

She kept her lashes lowered, cautioning herself to silence, as the gentleman stepped into the room and the doors were closed behind him.

Lord Stanley greeted him. "Lord Whitney, what a pleasant surprise. I'd planned to call on you myself, as soon as I'd heard you'd arrived. May I express my condolences for your father's passing. He was a distinguished gentleman, and a true friend. I assure you, he shall be missed by all."

Mylene felt the gentleman give a gracious bow.

"Allow me to present my good friend, Lord Helmsley. You'll be seeing a great deal of each other, I don't doubt."

The men shook hands.

"And this, sir, is my daughter, Mylene. Lord Whitney, from India."

Mylene set her face in courteous lines. But when she glanced up, the smile of welcome froze on her face.

It was Johnny!

On sale in September:

AFTER CAROLINE
by Kay Hooper

WHEN YOU WISH . . .
**by Jane Feather, Patricia
Coughlin, Sharon & Tom Curtis,
Elizabeth Elliot, Patricia Potter,
and Suzanne Robinson**

THE BARGAIN
by Jane Ashford

*THE CHALICE AND
THE BLADE*
by Glenna McReynolds

DON'T MISS THESE FABULOUS
BANTAM WOMEN'S FICTION TITLES

On Sale in August

DARK PARADISE

by TAMI HOAG,
The New York Times *bestselling author of* GUILTY AS SIN

A breathtakingly sensual novel filled with heart-stopping suspense and shocking passion . . . a story of a woman drawn to a man as hard and untamable as the land he loves, and to a town steeped in secrets—where a killer lurks. ____ 56161-8 $6.50/$8.99

THE MERMAID

by New York Times *bestseller* BETINA KRAHN,
author of THE UNLIKELY ANGEL

An enchanting new romance about a woman who works with dolphins in Victorian England and an academic who must decide if he will risk his career, credibility—and his heart—to side with the Lady Mermaid. ____ 57617-8 $5.99/$7.99

BRIDE OF DANGER

by KATHERINE O'NEAL,
winner of the Romantic Times *Award
for Best Sensual Historical Romance*

A spellbinding adventure about a beautiful spy who graces London's most elegant soirees and a devastatingly handsome rebel who asks her to betray everything she has come to believe in. ____ 57379-9 $5.99/$7.99

DON'T MISS THESE FABULOUS
BANTAM WOMEN'S FICTION TITLES